Stained Glass Myths

A Collection of Short Stories for Young Adults

Lune Spark Books, Apex, NC

Publisher: Lune Spark LLC

PO Box 1443, Morrisville, NC, 27560, United States

www.lunespark.com

Young Writers' Resources: www.lunespark.com/youngwriters

E-mail: books@lunespark.com

Phone: +1 (919) 809-4235

Hardback ISBN 13: 978-1-947960-35-0

Paperback ISBN 13: 978-1-947960-36-7

eBook ISBN 13: 978-1-947960-37-4

Cover art by Nishta Nandakumar

1. Short Stories 2. Anthology 3. Creative writing 4. Young writers

First edition

To the young writers who believe in their stories.

"There is no greater agony than bearing an untold story inside you."

—Maya Angelou

Introduction

In a short time, Lune Spark Short Story Contest has established itself as a unique platform for helping children hone their writing skills, learn the depth of the publishing process, and find other readers across the world through our yearly anthologies that are published internationally.

As of writing this, we have published stories from more than a hundred talented young writers. This contest has helped them experience what it takes to become a writer and the intricate process of publishing.

Similar to previous years, the stories this year show a tremendous amount of creativity and imagination. I feel proud to introduce yet another excellent anthology of stories by talented young writers! Wonderfully wide-ranging, original, and enjoyable, this outstanding collection features twenty-eight award-winning short stories.

My special gratitude goes to the following people. Running the contest and publishing this book couldn't have been possible without their help!

- The participants of the 2019 Lune Spark Short Story Contest and their parents for their high degree of engagement, enthusiasm, and support.
- The judges of the 2019 contest: Alexandra Williamson Hubbell, James Hockley, Jodie Reed, Pankaj Goyal, Rebecca McNutt, SF Benson, and Simon Brading. They helped us last year as well—their continued commitment to this cause is highly commendable!

Lastly, the best gift to a writer is a review. So let your take on their stories reach them in the form of a review anywhere you like—on a book website or on your blog. Rest assured that they will very eagerly be reading every single review, looking for encouragement and constructive criticism. Happy reading!

—Pawan Mishra, Apex, North Carolina
December 2019

Contents

Dear Rosemarie

Jordan Nelson

May 21, 1941

Dear Rosemarie,

It's your birthday today, Rosie. I was thinking about last year—I know, I know, a dangerous path to wander down—and I figured since we threw you a party then, that I should scrape one together for you now. Since you've been gone, I've grown up a little. You probably wouldn't recognize me if you saw me today. But God, I would give anything to see you right now. Your hair is most likely an inch or two longer, and it's curly now, right? Every year the tips curled a little, you hated—hate that. Oh, and you're going to be taller I bet. Maybe this will be the year you finally pass me in height. Sure, I'm three years younger than you, but I won't tell if you don't. Anything to make you happy.

Um, anyways, your party is sort of boring. Mom was always the one who decorated the house and you know I'm not good with heights. So I hung the banner I made at eye level. I hope you don't mind. I also kind of tore pages from your notebook to make the banner. Please don't get mad. And there's no cake. That was an obvious flaw to my plan. Cake batter and sprinkles have been absent here for a while. I'm sure that's not a surprise. Finding food has been pretty rough; they cut off the weekly supplies of bread to the house once you left. I think they believed that I would find somewhere else to stay now that I'm alone and I'm underage. But don't worry. I'm not going anywhere. This is our house.

A couple of people tried to evict me the other day because they needed the space more than I did apparently. Mrs. Alner helped me though. She convinced them to leave me alone. She's my favorite neighbor. She lives with Mr. Alner and her daughter Rebecca—remember her?—in a one-room house, and she's never asked to switch with me even though I've got the two-room one. Lucky me, right?

Okay, well, I just wanted to let you know what's been happening and maybe see if you would come home? I don't know where you are, but I'm sure it can't be as fun as being home with me, right? I miss you. Please write back.

Your little brother,
David

October 1, 1941

Dear Rosemarie,

Today's my birthday, Rosie. I'm thirteen. I didn't have a party. I figured it was stupid to celebrate something that doesn't really matter anymore, right? Oh, I wanted to apologize for my last letter. You never wrote back, and I'm guessing it's because I sounded so selfish. I feel like I let you down. You always tried to shape me into a good person, and I am very thankful for your help. But I won't lie to you. I'm also mad. Everyone kept me in the dark for so long, I'm surprised I haven't gone blind.

We're here because we're Jewish, but I still don't get it. Who cares what we believe in? Who cares if our thoughts are slightly different from everyone else? I want you to explain, Rosie. I need to know why. The people who took you, they were bad, weren't they? They weren't doctors. Everyone said that because you were sick, you were going to a hospital somewhere far away where you get ice cream before bed, and you can draw pictures with real crayons. But I know that's not true.

The other day, men came into the house. They were shouting bad things. Calling our home "dirty and disgusting" and saying we were "ungrateful worms." They wanted me to come with them, but I didn't

Rosie, I didn't. I hid in a cupboard until I couldn't hear their voices, and as soon as I knew they left, I ran over to Mrs. Alner's. And now her and her family live with me in our house. It's safer this way, and I have more food. But I didn't let them touch any of your stuff, Rosie. I promise.

I'm sorry this letter is filled with bad things, and I don't want you to be worried when you read this, but there's one more thing. I found out where you are. It's a place called Auschwitz. I wasn't supposed to hear the conversation, but I did. I still don't know what you're doing there though. You aren't very good at sewing, and I know you can't do any heavy lifting. That was always my job. Do you remember my ninth birthday? That's right. I'll never let you forget that day.

When you get this, please consider writing back. I feel stupid saying it, but I just need to see one word in your handwriting and I'll feel better. I want a hug too. I hope you're okay.

With love and hope,

David

January 14, 1942

Dear Rosemarie,

I don't think you're getting my letters. You haven't written back yet, and a small part of me believes that it's just because you don't have any paper in Auschwitz. I'm begging you, Rosie, please be out of writing materials. I need you to see these letters. I'm falling apart without you.

Do you remember the last snowfall we saw two years ago? It's a random question, I know, but I just realized that those were the final snowflakes we ever saw together. I was watching the snow this past December, and I found that snow is lonelier than you think. I mean no two snowflakes are alike. They all are alone just floating through the air with no purpose. But seeing those smiles on all those faces when inch upon inch of snow fell to the ground, I thought of you and how you would light up when you saw the coat of white that covered everything around us. Maybe snowflakes by themselves are lonely, but together the creation of snow is heartwarming.

Don't get mad, but, Rosie, I haven't eaten in three days. Rebecca and the other kids needed the bread more, and I'm like their big brother now as I'm the oldest in the ghetto. I tried to brush them off, but they're so innocent. These kids don't need to know what's happening around them, and I understand why you didn't allow me to know either. I'm sorry I got angry. If it makes you feel any better, I told them all about you. The youngest one, Eva, told me she wants to be just like you when she grows up. I nearly punched a man who said that she should've said "*if* she grows up." No one here is dying. Not Eva, not me, and certainly not you. Just hang in there, Rosie. I'll be there soon. I promise.

Please stay safe: for me, and Mom and Pop, and everyone we've lost.

Wishing for you always,
David

June 30, 1942

Dear Rosemarie,

You're dead, Rosie, aren't you?

You've been dead this whole time, right?

Auschwitz isn't a good place. It's not a hospital. It's not a ghetto. It's hell. Anyone who goes there dies, Rosie. Why, why did you have to get sick? You would be alive right now, reading these words, feeling the anger radiating off this page. You would see the tears that stain these last few pieces of paper I have left. I won't be writing anymore. There's no point.

The lead in my pencil is almost gone, and my ability to sit still enough and write meaningless sentences and mail meaningless letters has worn thin.

After a long day of corralling children into their homes, Mrs. Alner tiredly whispered under her breath, "Acting like this, these children will end up gassed at Auschwitz," and I lost everything, Rosie, *everything*. Sure, she wasn't thinking when she said it, but it doesn't change the fact that I know.

You were going to be seventeen this year. I would have gathered all the children to celebrate your day, and we would've all been happy. But that never happened. Your day came and went, and after it went, it died. May 21 is just another pointless stretch of time that we all have to sit through, tired and hungry.

I'm scared, Rosie. There's less than twenty of us here. So my last letter actually rang true in one way: I'll see you soon.

Sincerely,

David

The Narrative Traveler

Max Dreyfuss

The past is a foreign country; they do things differently there. The timeless saying kept bouncing around in my mind as I stepped into my time machine, setting the controls to take me to the end of the story.

With a puff of metatextual smoke I was off, whizzing between sentences and paragraphs at the speed of bad writing. Where was I even getting these little quips, and why was I bothering to make them? I mentally shook my fist at whoever was writing me, then focused my attention back on piloting my time machine. I was just planning on popping into the end of the story and grabbing a snack or two, then heading back to the beginning. Of course, I had to admit that things were rarely that simple in a story like the one I lived in…

And sure enough, I had made a small miscalculation in my destination. My time machine glanced off an errant group of sentences and went into a mad spin, everything inside the machine bouncing off everything else. My head was included in this, and I had become intimately familiar with the experience of being a sock in a washing machine by the time I finally landed.

I crawled out of the smoldering wreckage of my time machine, struggled to my feet, and looked around. I was in an unfamiliar paragraph that didn't look anything like the ending. I heaved a sigh—my time machine was totaled, so my only hope was to make my way back to the beginning of the story and steal my own time machine from myself. And I was almost certainly miles away from the beginning, since that was where I had just come from. I resolved to trek all the way back and started gathering supplies from the paragraph I was currently in. It looked like some giant robots were for some reason currently fighting a giant spider far off in the distance, but that had nothing to do with me, so I finished getting supplies and started on my backward journey.

As I trekked through the story, the plot revealed itself to me in reverse. It all struck me as incredibly bland, boring, and pointless. I wondered what kind of talentless hack was writing this story and what idiot would ever read it. Much better to stick around near the beginning where things were simple and quiet.

Finally, gleaming off in the distance like the gleam of a terribly written simile, I saw the beginning of the story. I ran full-speed toward it. I had to get there before I took off in my time machine for the ending!

I saw myself at last, about to step into my time machine. With no other options, I tackled myself at full force, knocking myself away from the door. He jumped up and shook his fist angrily at me. "You idiot! Don't you realize that by doing that, you've created a paradox and doomed us both?!"

I cursed myself for my mistake, but it was too late—the me that had been tackled to the ground was vanishing into nothingness as his timeline stopped existing. All my memories faded until I remembered nothing about what I had just gone through. The paragraphs vanished—it was like I had never trekked through them. In erasing the other me, I had started the story over, and I didn't even remember it.

The past is a foreign country; they do things differently there. The timeless saying kept bouncing around in my mind as I stepped into my time machine, setting the controls to take me to the end of the story.

Backpacks

Huda Haque

Some people didn't want to recover the bags from the school. Why would they? They were items that witnessed mass murder, a tragedy of incomprehensible sorts. They were stained with the anguished screams of teenagers and the maddening finality of bullets. What actually mattered, after something that catastrophic happened?

This question buzzed through my head as I walked toward the pile of backpacks that lay on the school grounds, yet I couldn't answer it; I was simply too numb. The backpacks lay together in a silent mass of eerie memories as more and more students tore away from the crowds and police cars and observed them.

I wasn't quite sure what I was looking for. My own backpack? No, it was impossible to find it, and at the moment, I felt as if looking at it would make me crumble. The entirety of the past few hours was a shaky blur, yet the memory of my bag underneath my trembling fingers as bullets ricocheted was crystal clear. The mere thought of revisiting that made me shiver with an icy fear. Instead, I walked along the pile, looking for any shred of familiarity I could discern. Then a muted lilac pattern caught my eye. It was recognizable to me in an instant. Lucie's. There it lay, the backpack I stared at during first period every day, and the backpack I was staring at when the first bullet rang through the hallways. My hands subconsciously went toward it among the pile, and I mindlessly thumbed over the myriad of key chains adorning the bag. They were all from different countries, and suddenly memories of Lucie twirling her chocolate-brown hair around her finger while enthusiastically telling me of her travels came rushing back. A stained, crumpled piece of paper stuck out of the backpack, and I could slightly make out the title: *Travel Bucket List.* The three words were sprawled in a glittery, faded ink. Numbness overtook me as I recalled her dream to visit every country in the world in her lifetime, and how the last thing she saw in that lifetime instead were the shattered, bloodstained glass panes of our classroom door. I stiffened and quickly looked through the pile again.

This time, a navy-blue bag stood out to me. It was beaten up, considerably more than the rest of the backpacks. You could make out the sharp spikes poking through the well-worn fabric. Cleats. I squinted, trying to place where I had seen it before, when someone noticed me staring at it.

"That was Jack's," the other student said quietly, and even though it was a mere three words, I could hear the shaking tremble of her voice. "The kid who would help everyone."

"Oh. Oh, of course, yeah. I remember," I replied quickly, not wanting to betray my shock.

Jack was lauded as the smartest kid in our grade and was often found dropping everything just to answer your question. Not only that, but he was a star soccer player and traveled to less-funded elementary schools just to teach kids how to play. He was known for his killer left foot, and I hazily remembered seeing a flash of it wounded earlier as he flailed and screamed on a stretcher. The boy who ran, kicked, and scored through life, and now we weren't sure if he would walk again. All because of those few minutes. Gulping in air, I started moving along the pile.

I spotted a different type of bag this time, and I remembered exactly where I saw it last. That was the weird thing—in the midst of grief, I recalled oddly specific details. The bag had been swinging off the shoulder of the man holding the hefty school doors open for us while we had desperately run outside hours earlier. It hadn't belonged to a student, but a teacher. The art teacher, Mr. Abbott.

I closed my eyes as the memory floated back to

me.

"RUN! COME ON!" he screamed, the bag swinging furiously as he motioned toward us. The memory continued until my mind got to the worst part—the eventual closing of the doors as he suddenly collapsed while screams and bullets rained.

Pain seized me, and my eyes snapped open in an instant, settling back on his bag. The material was quite simple, made of a cream-white fabric, but its canvas was filled with stickers and buttons. Most of them sung praises about the joy of teaching, some were professional, and others were handmade.

Looking closer, I saw one of the handmade ones said, "Mr. Abbott—Best Teacher Ever!" The moment I realized the polka dots on it were actually blood was the moment I remembered more about Mr. Abbott. He was the same teacher who was known to spend his lunch break talking with lonely students. He was the same teacher who gave a vivacious smile to everyone he passed in the hallway. And now, he was the teacher who would never walk those hallways again.

Suddenly, I felt faint staring at the bloodied buttons, so I tore my gaze away to the pile once more as tears swam in my eyes, the bags doubling in the wash of them. I was now aware of the group of people around me, a crowd, actually. Some of them were parents, but most were students. They all had the same glazed-over look as their eyes pored over the bags, not knowing what they were searching for. Up until now, I hadn't really spoken to any of them, instead choosing to observe in an intense silence, blocking out the others around me. Then, a tap on my shoulder.

"I—I saw y-your backpack. Just...if you wanted it. It's over here."

After whirling around, I stared at the source of the voice, which turned out to be one of my classmates. "Really?" I said. "Can you show me it?"

I was surprised by my own new willingness to see my backpack. My classmate led me to it. There it was. The trusty bag I stuffed my homework in every day, the bag I excitedly put key chains on, and finally the bag I prayed would shield me from bullets. Looking at it suddenly overwhelmed me, and I shakily stepped back, seeing the bags again, but this time in a different light.

They were no longer just that, no longer simply objects, but instead the victims and survivors themselves. They embodied our unwavering compassion, humanity, and hope. They encapsulated our experiences and showed how our strength carried us in the horrifying moments we had witnessed. A single tear ran down my cheek, but this time it glistened with clarity. We were all so much more than those few minutes, so much more than the hatred that furiously tried to strike us down. I took a deep breath and curled my hand into a determined fist, silently making a vow.

I wouldn't let our actions and spirits be lost. And I would work to make sure this wouldn't happen. Never again.

Lidia's Letter

Huda Haque

"We'll be waiting out here, okay?" my parents say as they shut my door.

"Okay! I have a feeling that this'll be my best birthday gift yet!" I reply excitedly.

The aftermath of my eighteenth birthday party—crumpled streamers and loose glitter—lay as silent witnesses to me fiddling with the metallic box in my room, darkened by the quiet night outside.

"EARTH 2, 2019 | RECIPIENT: LIDIA JAMES" it reads in a turquoise glow.

It feels as if all my life has been leading up to this moment. This is going to be my turning point. At least, that's what I have been telling myself in the past. Finally being able to open my Letter…finally being able to know what the future me from Earth 1 wrote…it would mean my unsure life would surely get back on track. It would mean that I wouldn't just be the same aimless, confused teenager running in circles anymore. That's what everyone told me. My parents and older friends all reassured me that my Letter would tell me something valuable. For their own Letters, they received practical advice, what regrets to undo, or something in that vein. Whatever it was—it made their lives much better. That was the point of the Letter System: give people on our Earth a better life.

How? Centuries ago, an alliance was forged between the parallel worlds of Earth 1 and my home, Earth 2. We all have counterparts there who have the exact same lives, except they age much, much faster. When our Earth 1 equivalents feel old enough, they write a mandatory beneficial Letter to us to read on our eighteenth birthday.

So here I am, with the box that holds that Letter. I trace my finger along the steel engravings of it, inhaling deeply. *There's nothing to be gained by drawing it out,* I tell my anxious self. Finally, after undoing the clasps with shaky fingers and thrusting the top open, I look into the ominous box that holds my future.

"AAAAHHH!" My blood-curdling scream sends my parents scrambling into my room.

"What happened?" they yelp.

I look up frantically. "T-there's nothing! It's empty! There's no Letter!"

"What do—did you drop it?"

"No! I just opened it!"

The room swims before my eyes. How could this

be happening? It's a question I repeat several times mindlessly as Mom turns the house upside down and Dad messes with the box.

Our fruitless attempts continue for hours, until birds start abruptly chirping outside as the sun rises. It's a sign to stop. I sigh and tuck my hands in my pockets.

"We've searched enough. It's not here."

My words have a tinge of annoyance in them, although I try to conceal it. I've been waiting for this Letter for eighteen years, and now it doesn't show up?

"What do I even do now?" I ask hopelessly.

"Well…I guess you go to the Letter Headquarters and ask them," Dad replies slowly.

Huffing, I grab my car keys off my desk. "You guys stay here. You've done more than enough."

My parents eye each other worriedly. "Lidia, you sure?" Mom asks.

I hesitate in the doorway, but then realize that this is hopefully going to be my first step toward an independent, better life. "Yeah. I think it's my responsibility."

Some responsibility this was shaping up to be. Cars shrieked their protests among the crowded roads, and my temples throbbed as I pulled into HQ.

Much to my annoyance, sweat beaded down my forehead and hair, no doubt ensuring I would look like a messy kid when I arrived. They probably would think I was joking, and my hurried clothing choice (graphic T-shirt and ripped jeans) didn't help. In spite of all of that, though, I knew I needed this Letter more than anything. I saw the impact it had on my friends' lives—whether it be them moving to a different place or applying for a job. My Letter had to be that golden key for me. Because if it wasn't, I would have to accept the fact that my life had to be carved out by just me, without the help every single person I knew had gotten in the form of their Letters. And that possibility was too unnerving to confront.

That's what I repeated to myself as I walked into HQ. The tall, monolithlike appearance of the daunting glass doors would usually send me running in the other direction, but I had too much to lose. So I strode up to the receptionist, my sneakers squeaking on the impeccably white floors. "Hello. Yesterday was my eighteenth birthday, and I didn't receive my Letter."

The receptionist peers through spectacles and coughs arduously. "You're sure ya didn't toss it somewhere?" she sniffs.

"Yes, ma'am."

"Fine, go over to that back door and ask for Jack."

I nod and scurry over to the door, where I ask the burly security guard about the Jack in question. He swings the door open silently, and we walk down a narrow white hallway.

"In here," the guard says gruffly, and I'm suddenly pushed into a room.

The door slams shut behind me with an air of finality as I yelp, "Hey!"

Someone in the depths of the room laughs, and my face starts reddening. All of a sudden, that same uneasiness starts overtaking me, and I can feel myself struggling for words. It turns out I don't need them, as the someone who laughed at my surprise steps forward and starts talking.

"Ms. James? I'm Jack Weiss, director of Letter management. What seems to be the problem?"

The voice belongs to a handsome young man with a sweep of dark chestnut hair and matching eyes, crinkled in amusement. He doesn't seem much older than me. Maybe his Letter told him which career path to follow.

I look up at his smiling face, then nervously back down at my feet. "I—I didn't get my Letter yesterday. I'm really worri—" I stammer, suddenly acutely aware of exactly what could happen if I don't get my Letter. My life would fall apart.

Jack places a hand on my shoulder warmly. "It's okay, Lidia. I'll scan your ID, and we'll get you the Letter. It's probably just a glitch."

I sigh with relief, even though I've never heard of a glitch happening. "I know, I've just been waiting for so long…it's kind of my lifeline."

He smiles comfortingly, then takes my ID to a large station lit in a turquoise glow. I carefully watch him as he pushes buttons and scans my ID, not knowing what I'm waiting for. Suddenly, I hear a "beep," and my heart starts throbbing. What does it mean? I can hardly breathe when I see Jack's expression change from confident to confused. He purses his lips, then slowly walks over to me.

"I'm so sorry," he starts. "Lidia—"

No, no, it can't be, I think. *This can't happen.*

"There's no Letter for you."

Then everything fades to black.

EIGHTY YEARS LATER: EARTH 2 | 2099

My breathing has slowed now, much like the rest of me. I look out of my luxurious bedroom, decorated with "HAPPY BIRTHDAY" balloons, at the turquoise ocean that is my front yard, and smile. My demeanor now is a far cry from that of the nervous teenager I used to be. It took a while for me to get over not having a Letter. Years, actually. I might not have gotten out of that slump if it wasn't for the person sitting next to me now. He told me I was more than enough without that piece of paper and made me realize I didn't need someone else to make my life better. That job was mine, and mine alone.

"What are you smiling about?" he asks, laughing.

"Oh, nothing, Jack. Do you remember when I was so upset about not getting a Letter?"

Jack starts to speak but is cut off by a knocking on the door.

"Mom!" My daughter flies in. "This was just delivered!"

She's holding a box exactly the same as the one I fiddled with years ago. I sit upright, then look at Jack. "Do you remember anything like this ever happening?"

"No, not in the sixty years I worked for HQ…open the box!"

I do and gasp. It's a Letter.

Dear Lidia,

I'm sure you were upset on your eighteenth birthday. I hope you've forgiven me! You see, I watched others around me write Letters to people on your Earth, knowing that just their words would alter lives forever. I didn't want that for you. I remember feeling lost, confused, but still yearning for the day I would learn how to be independent. Just as you did. And when I got to old age, I realized, I couldn't bring myself to take that yearning away from you. Sending a Letter would be taking away your opportunity to see the beauty that is the unknown, to realize that it's okay to not know where your path leads. So I arranged for your Letter to be sent later, after you got to understand that for yourself. I hope you realize that was my first gift to you all those years ago, and this Letter now is my last gift.

Sincerely,
Lidia James of Earth 1

I fold up the letter, wiping away a tear. Jack and my daughter are staring at me.

"So what is it?" my daughter asks.

Smiling, I respond, "It's my second best birthday gift yet."

We Are Free

Elliot Hui

Brothers

Thirty famished bodies jostled against one another in a tight huddle. Despite being prisoners, we pushed past our captors' unrelenting hatred. Blows have rained down before, yet today we face indescribable horrors. Our strength is waning.

With every stubborn rock in the road, we became ragdolls trapped in an iron crate on wheels. All in one violent motion, bony elbows cracked against nearby ribs and skinned knees smashed into the bruised faces of others. When one of us cried out, a S.S. guard would rise from the front of the car and unleash a fiery hail of bullets toward the ashen sky. The thunderous automatic weaponry muffled his commands for us to be quiet. As pungent fumes of gunpowder floated overhead, we cowered within the box, haunted by the sounds that brought the end of our dreams even closer. Soon I found myself buried among other prisoners. Each covered their faces with soiled caps, begging for the slightest sign of mercy.

"Meir, where are you?" my brother called.

The six-year-old's feeble voice was drowned out by neighboring cries of terror. His stubby hand poked out between someone's back and another's lap, fingers searching for me.

My ears perked up at proof of the only other living soul that mattered.

"Here, brother, how are you?" I responded, trembling with concern.

I moved toward the sound of his voice, but not before the gap between us was filled by several bodies that rushed in. We were all suffocating; nobody cared who stood in their way. Space was air, and air was time.

"Do you remember when we had picnics?" He coughed, dust filling his lungs.

"Yes, Adam. Those were lovely."

My teenage mind drifted off into the past, floating away from the chaos. Away from the day Father was shot, away from the day Mother was lost in the Selection. Adam and I longed for Mother's caring touch, but neither of us knew where she was now. Since then we only had each other.

Gasping more than breathing, Adam managed to sob, "Meir, I am scared."

Silence.

I dove toward him with both arms outstretched. I could not lose my brother. Not now.

"*When*" was the very word that kept me clinging to life, refusing to surrender my brother's well-being. I kept repeating the word, envisioning all the light I would see beyond bales of barbed wire.

Gritting my teeth, I questioned the world. "*When* will we return home?" I slid across the rusted wall of our suffocating jail.

"*When* will we see Mother again?" My innocence pleaded for freedom while my defiant youth demanded I fight for this family. I clawed and scratched a path to Adam, thrashing in a sea of melancholy. Deprived of hope, we all slowly drowned in the stale air.

"*When?*" Just four inches from him.

"*When?*" Two inches.

"*When?*" One.

At last I wrapped my hand around his. A crippling fear brought me to my knees as I traced Adam's clammy skin. I watched his concave chest rising and falling just a hair. He faintly squeezed back in a struggle to maintain consciousness.

The jingling of keys from outside brought a wave of silence over us all. Footsteps shuffled toward the back of the car. The glimmer of hope that briefly shone on our grimy faces washed away faster than it appeared. Our sunken eyes sank even farther in an unnerving brew of confusion and fear.

"Wherever we end up," I rasped, folding my ill brother over my shoulders. "Nothing can ever separate us."

A Mirage

The screaming doors to our transport flung open on corroded hinges. The light I had prayed for was absent in the dead air. Freedom was only a painful mirage. On the other side were not our families who welcomed us home with open arms, but a grimacing S.S. Army.

"Move! I don't care if you're tired, move!" ordered the first guard, lips contorted with repulsion. His pupils were flamethrowers of their own, staring each of us down in the night.

Broken from our petrified stances, our muscles snapped into coordination one by one. We spilled out of the car in a dysfunctional dance of forced mechanical movements. Crumpled on the damp grass, I gulped the whistling countryside breeze. I then raised my head to face our desolate surroundings. Endless rolling plains was another jail in itself; a maze nobody could escape. Dead trees were sporadically placed with withered branches home to a dozen crows. Their silhouettes greedily craved my emaciated corpse, beaks twitching impatiently. Others circled beneath the clouds and let out a deafening caw every time they neared. Rancid bile came up at the thought of them waiting to feast.

Surrounding soldiers gave a series of shoves, funneling us toward to the top of the nearest grass hill. Thousands of similarly bewildered prisoners followed our lead. The transports' gaseous engines roared a rude farewell as they raced away.

An elderly man rose up in protest, throwing down his checkered prisoner's cap. "We need a place to rest!"

"You all can rest here," a guard sneered. "Permanently."

He was thrown along. Confidence in the guard's chilling words turned my blood cold. I carried my brother a little higher.

Farewell

We marched on, braving the frigid winds. At last we stood upon the lonely hill, not a single sign of hope to be seen. A shrill voice rang out from behind.

"Halt! All of you, kneel!"

With a clatter, rifles leveled against our chests and realization struck all of us at once. Some cried and prayed. Others closed their eyes.

"I will not bow," I declared. This time my voice did not quiver. Oppressors and oppressed, everyone turned my way. My skeletal frame slowly rose to a stand.

"Stop!" the guard bellowed.

Soldiers adjusted their grips with sweaty palms, unmistakable fear plastered across their faces. When they finally managed to chamber a round, each trained their iron barrels on the weapon I possessed. My defiance.

The Uprising

"Your words don't intimidate me!" I shouted.

The rural wind seemed to swirl around my battered figure, casting my words down the rolling plains. I had broken the silence. From the summit of the grassy mound, I looked down onto our captors—a scattered array of onyx helmets that glared back at me.

"Last chance! Obey!" the guard warned, his voice rising in pitch.

His words were powerless when pitted against mine. A lion among a field of sheep, my spirit had transcended all that stood in its way. I rose above as an example for fellow prisoners to follow. I planted my foot firmly on the hill.

The guard trembled with rage knowing his words meant nothing. He lowered his head, shaking a white-knuckled fist. From his tantrum, the powerless S.S. guard motioned to his comrades. Steel-toe boots raced about as they kicked up dirt, braided laces whipping the grass. Beads of dew flew astray. With a flurry of brisk hand signals and shouts, the S.S. quickly formed an impenetrable circle around us. All means of escape were sealed off, except for one: the sky above us. We, the prisoners, were no longer captive.

"Aghh!"

Our attention swiveled. The elder among us who had made the painful sound paused to lick his lips. He then let out a dying father's cry again and again. Agonizing cries rolled down from the hills, blending into a song of sorrow. A mother of two followed suit. Her children clapped along, hips swaying to the climbing beat. The crows had flown away.

Now all the prisoners sang in harmony, spirits rising for their broken dreams. Our hoarse voices and strained lyrics filled the night, fighting the oncoming gunfire. Even as our bodies fell with a muted thud, we could not be silenced. Their weapons had reigned terror over many miles, yet our song could be heard for eternity.

"Meir," a fading voice called.

I peered down. My baby brother lay sprawled on the ground, a victorious smile growing on his pallid face. Tears welled up in the corners of my eyes as he mouthed three words.

"*We are free.*"

I did not flinch as the guard facing me began to pull his trigger. I took my first breath of freedom.

Color-Blind

Charlotte Flynn

There is this boy. A boy I once knew. One that I used to play with. He was the ragged kind; the one that shoved you to the side to get to the toy first, or kicked at the dirt to see it fly, or fell out of a tree and scraped his arms. I didn't mind. I followed along, picking up the toy that he didn't grab, grasping at the grains of dirt that flew in the air, staring from the branches of the tree at him on the ground. He seemed carefree. Like nothing could hurt him. And even when he *was* injured, he brushed it off like it was nothing. I admired his strength. We played like good friends, and our memories made their imprint in our minds, in our hearts.

I saw in color. The brilliant hues paint the world different shades of beauty. I could see the trees shake their leafy green heads as they toss in the wind, and the blue of oceans that churn and send their waves crashing down on the beach. The yellow of the sun and its fiery beams lighting earth, and the red of the roses that unfurl their delicate petals and bloom in the spring. I saw God's paintbrush at work; careful strokes filling us with each of our own light.

I saw that light in him. This boy I once knew. The kind of light that means you were born to stand out. I saw it reflected in his piercing blue eyes, the kind of eyes that can look into your soul and delve for the truth. It shone from his light skin and radiated from his dark curls. When he smiled, it was as if that light ignited from his heart and made its way onto his face. He emanated so many different colors and hues it was as if a rainbow had made its delicate strokes across his soul.

The world saw in black and white.

They saw only two kinds of people. The light and the dark. People with faces pale like the moon and people with faces like the night sky. They did not see the shades in between, or the tints that nature painted around them. Their minds were closed to the colors of creation, sealed and turned away from the inspiration of the world around them.

His father was among their numbers.

He had always been a shadow upon us, a looming menace that darkened our memories. His eyes were a colorless gray that peered coldly down at me, sneering. He had never liked me much, and it angered him when he saw me with his son. The anger was laced with fear, as if I would influence his precious boy to commit serious offenses. As if I was responsible for the evils in the world, and I would infect his son like a disease, tainting his mind with corrupt thoughts.

I remember the way he would walk, a slow limping shuffle. He would come outside and yell slurred language at us in the same stained shirt every day, his neck red with sunburn and in his hands a brown bottle filled with amber liquid. Whenever he made an appearance, the boy's eyes grew cloudy and somber, and his mouth formed into a line as if he was waiting for him to deliver a penalty. It was my nature to comfort, but he pushed me away, the ragged edges of his personality refusing any solace. He was a kinder spirit than his father, and he could see the shades of gray between the sharp divide of white and black. His father had been so keen on keeping us apart it only drove us closer together.

I didn't know it would lead to violence. I didn't know his father was so unstable and filled with hate he inflicted his wrath upon his only son. There was no mother to stop him; as far as I knew she had never existed. I would see the bruises on his pale arm, and my soft brown hands would try to soothe his pain. His mask of strength was cracking, and the fear of his father grew. We stopped playing at his house. My backyard was smaller, but we continued to have our adventures, despite the strife, despite the color of our skin. My comfort healed him if only briefly.

Then one day, the boy I once knew was gone.

His father seemed to have uprooted him from our town and left. The house was empty. I had grown to dislike the house; the constant apprehension and the stench of alcohol plaguing the inside of its walls. Now I resented it even more; it had been bearable with the sound of our laughter bouncing down the corridors, but now silence bore upon me so fiercely that it rang in my ears. The boy was gone, the light of his spirit gone with him. I told my mother of his departure. She placed my head in her hands and wrapped her strong brown arms around me.

"You pray for that boy. Pray that he finds peace wherever he is. Pray for his father too. So he becomes a better man. To his son, to our people, and to others around him."

"Yes, Momma," I whispered into her ear, and she hugged me tighter.

I hoped one day he and others like him would learn it was a matter of feeling with the heart instead of seeing with the eyes. I prayed every night. I never stopped praying for the boy and his father. I prayed so they could find peace and at last live the lives they wanted. I prayed for them and everyone else struggling for a chance to prosper.

I am still praying.

There is this girl. This girl I once knew. One that I used to play with. She was the gentle kind; the one that soothed your hurt and sorrow, or sang little songs in a high clear key, or patiently listened with a big heart while you spoke. I saw her for how she was—a little girl with a kind soul and a caring nature. There was a spark in her that flared to life when she smiled, and she was so full of life it was as if she drank sunbeams and they ignited in her eyes.

My father saw differently.

He never saw beyond her skin color. Her dark complexion filled his small heart with hate despite her kind and generous nature. He thought he was better. He believed he was the superior person because he was a male with white skin. I didn't want to think that way, but living in the same house as him made it hard not to adopt his ideologies. I would push the girl away when those thoughts launched into my mind, but seeing her so caring and sweet made it hard for them to stay. My father was my superior, but I couldn't adopt his beliefs because they were just *wrong.* The alcohol made him rage, and although it strengthened his anger, it also strengthened his fear. He screamed at me for playing with her and slapped me when I argued. He was a terrible man, and I lived in fear of him.

I was stronger than he was. He was color-blind, only seeing in black and white. I could see between the lines, and there was beauty everywhere. My upbringing didn't stop me from seeing the truth. We are one people. It doesn't matter where we come from or what we look like; we are the same. My father never stopped to think about that. If I could see the girl one more time, I would say I'm sorry. For my father's ignorance and for everyone else who thought the same way he did. She inspired me to see with all the colors instead of black and white. She didn't even know it.

One time, I heard a voice whisper in the air.

"Please God, be with him and show him the kindness he deserves. Help his father be a better man."

I didn't know how, but I knew it was her. She was whispering to help me, to mend my broken spirit. Despite the backlash she received in return for being my companion, she prayed for me. I smiled; one day the divide between white and black would piece itself back together and we would be whole again. The hatred would dissipate in its own revolting cloud of smoke, and the world and its people would be at peace. Not all stories end happily, but at least they end with a promise of relief and reprieve. The thought gave me comfort, and the girl flashed across my mind one last time. One day we would have our chance.

One day.

Earth as Home

Jona David Cordonier-Gehring

We gasped in awe as the observatory deck opened, and we first glimpsed the stained-glass streaks of Earth's azure and emerald jewel through the churning cauldron of charcoal clouds and mercury mists. The commander of the International Space Station, standing before the Winchester College first-year students, paused expectantly. "Any questions?" he asked in a wise and gentle voice.

Immediately five of our classmates' hands shot up, punching through the frozen air of the space chamber. "Why are those dark clouds still encircling our planet?" was the first question.

"It was all due to the climate crisis all those years ago," the commander solemnly replied.

"Our teachers have told us about how terrible climate change became, with the endless storms, floods. and other extreme weather… still, as someone who actually experienced the conditions himself, who lived through it all, was it truly so difficult?" I asked in a quiet whisper.

"It almost turned the world into a crucible of chaos and catastrophe," the commander explained patiently. "When I was only slightly older than you, our entire civilization came within a whisper of apocalypse."

Everyone leaned closer across the gleaming titanium rails, as the storms continued roiling far, far beneath us.

"We saw entire countries sinking beneath murky waves. Countless chaotic typhoons clawed angrily at our fragile cities, destroying the homes of millions of people," the commander further explained. "Even by 2020, our scientists had already found multiple solutions. However, many governments could not remain committed to the necessary long-term plans and constraints, rendering them essentially ephemeral. As soon as governments changed, their pristine promises shattered like glass snowflakes in a surging storm. At first, the most powerful people disregarded the facts, attempting to hide behind their cast-iron gates as wildfires began to burn around them. At its most extreme, climate change brought nearly one-third of countries into lost, tattered, and sunken ruins. Close to one-fifth of the world's people almost starved in refugee camps of patchwork tents and makeshift shelters. The challenge was truly our generation's race against extinction." The commander gazed seriously down to the gleaming jewel of the Earth that hung below us, suspended against the blazing radiance of the stars.

A deafening silence fell, as the commander's firm

yet frightening words sunk solemnly into our souls. All we could hear was the quiet whirring of the artificial quantum flux gravity generators, as the International Space Station spun in its orbit.

Finally, my friend Edward mustered the courage to ask, in a hushed yet serious tone, "In that case, sir… why do any of us exist at all?"

The commander turned back to us, an almost joyful gleam in his eyes. "It is actually due to students just like you. As early as 2019, climate strikes were held, at first every month, all across the globe. The students mobilized peaceful yet compelling arguments and action—teach-ins, petitions, marches, and vigils. They knew that if they did not find a way to stop the climate emergency, they would be the last generation to ever walk the Earth. In essence, the students were standing up for humanity itself, and with it, our entire planet."

"Didn't they think you were insane?" one of the boys asked, with genuine concern. "How could a few young people possibly stop the weather itself, or bring about the profound economic transformations that were needed?"

"Yes, however, we knew that if we could not begin at that time, no matter how hopeless, there would be no second chance. Some governments still did ignore us, of course. It took an entire generation, at first resisting, but then also learning and innovating together. Just before the crisis became too great, the younger generation—who had once been silenced and reviled—finally took up scientific and political leadership of the already-stormy world.

Thankfully, we remembered our commitments and came together," the commander added. "The political leaders did their part, rallying the populations and keeping the priorities clear. But it was the scientists and innovators, those former students, who also stepped up. The biologists were crucial—their velvet strands of soft sage-hued bioengineered carbon-consuming moss clung to every stark concrete surface. Spidery olive-green fronds of oxygenating aerophytes carpeted and eventually converted all the iron infrastructure. Bridges, buildings, highways, and overpasses crumbled, even as we frantically rebuilt with lighter carbon-neutral materials. The chemists and engineers turned their imaginations wild as well—their renewable nanobots and graphite piping structured new sustainable transport systems all over the world at hypersonic speeds, mitigating and eventually eliminating the exorbitant travel and shipping emissions. And for us, the physicists? With the help of the ISS, we chose the steepest, rockiest battlefield at the pinnacle of the problem itself."

I could not contain my joyful shout. "Energy, sir!"

"Precisely," replied the commander with a gleaming spark in his eyes. "We finally harnessed the cores of stars—fusion power. By combining all our efforts, the climate crisis was considered closed by 2064. Innovation had—just barely—allowed the people of our precious yet polluted planet to turn together away from the brink of extinction toward a new, and now nearly thriving world."

We all watched as the clouds slowly parted just a little farther, and a little more of our home was revealed. Everyone else stayed riveted.

But Edward and I, as endlessly imaginative as our ancestors, couldn't help looking farther out, far from humanity's first sanctuary, toward the distant diamonds of the universe's unexplored expanse.

"A home," I whispered to him, "is the place from which one begins the voyage."

As we returned together to Earth, changed, each student from the class integrated our new understandings into our lives in different ways.

For Edward and me, a Cambridge Pre-University science project became our first faltering steps toward our greatest achievement. It began one day when we were reflecting on our tour on the ISS in those early years, when we had been so much in awe of the distant stars:

"Remember all those scientists the commander mentioned? I've been wondering—why couldn't we also do something for the future of humanity?" I started.

"But everything has already been solved. Climate change has been laid to rest, and the inefficient, profligate mega-corporations have been disassembled," Edward pessimistically replied.

"Yes, but maybe… remember my idea, right after the commander's speech?"

"You're a genius! But how could we possibly figure out how to travel to other star systems?"

"Well, we can't move faster than light—but perhaps we can bend it, just enough to pass through!" I exclaimed.

It began as small collection of equipment in the workshop; however, the project soon consumed our scientific research careers. We both graduated, but continued to spend long hours, then weeks, then months, ensconced in the clear chrome crucible of our Oxford physics laboratory. Together, we struggled with the very limits of the space-time continuum, secure in the friendship that we had formed during that fateful ISS field visit, but constantly failing to make the one last step that might bring our dreams into reality.

One evening, frustrated beyond belief, we stormed out from our containment fields into the sage-green fenland meadows behind our lab. We pushed through the heavy, humid air and the draping willow fronds, to find a quiet sage-green clearing.

And in the soft green twilight of the fens, we paused.

Iridescent eyes, ancient and alien, reflected our cautious smiles. Across thirty-five million years of survival, a strange winged being stared back at us, eerily reminiscent of our wise commander's gaze. We both gasped with shared awe, as the peculiar creature hovered higher, then flew away over the swathes of wetland reeds and rushes.

With a shared glance and a grin, we followed, clambering onward over the soft lichen-coated stones that bubbled up across the marshes, tracking the elusive insect, until we came to a translucent pool. There, the glimmering dragonfly hovered, silently extending its quartered translucent wings, its pearlescent eyes observing us both as shivers crept up our spines. In the strange hum of its wings, we suddenly grasped the shining idea that could solve our entire project. Just as we turned to each other to explain, astonished and excited, the creature flashed with light, then faded into a brief, fragile emerald speck and disappeared across the fens.

We raced back to the lab.

Reaching into our virtual prototype, I connected the gravitational distortion engine to the hyperdrive, this time recycling the warp-thrust generated inward upon itself and allowing us to harness a compact form of nearly limitless energy. It was almost as though, once we truly understood that waste was neither necessary nor possible, we could finally overcome the conceptual barriers that had held us down. The new gravitational wave reactor was born!

We had no idea what to do next, so I wrote to ISS, to the commander who first inspired us. Fortunately, he supported our proposal. Work began in earnest.

A few years later, even as the heavy pewter and charcoal clouds slowly cleared from our Earth's sky, finally ending the last vestiges of the climate emergency, we delivered on our promise. After all the trials and experiments, it was our prototype that finally resolved the interstellar light-speed cap for space travel. Together, Edward and I finished the capsule, and with a great deal of help (and no small ceremony) from other ISS scientists, we set off toward the distant stars.

In a distorted instant, our destination neared—the brilliant and elusive Proxima-B, closest planet to the

Earth that might be capable of sustaining life. As our gravitational hyperdrive capsule hovered, then streaked toward the surface, I peered out across the roiling shadows to the stained-glass jewel hues of the planet below and felt a strange sense of déjà vu.

I turned to my friend Edward, companion and coconspirator from the start. "Does something seem familiar to you?"

He nodded as the vehicle softly settled and the shrouds of murmuring mists parted.

Our viewscreen cleared, and a delirious viridian everglade towered around us, carpeted with warped wetland wildflowers and willowlike fronds, bending with immense yet wispy ferns. As the onboard air samples registered, and the all-clear was issued for human breath, together we opened our outer airlock and clambered down to the field below.

Three glinting, shimmering figures were approaching on soaring wings, gradually emerging from the emerald mists with a familiar hum. We knew not whether it was joy or terror in our hearts, as we once again met the ancient dragonfly's curious, iridescent gaze and heard, as a soft sigh on the whispering wind, its nearly silent welcome.

Loose Morales

Anuksha Madhan

We find that war, akin to many such things, is often absurd and pointless.

Butcherous, bloody, and baneful, war is often an unnecessary response to a problem easily solved in alternative manners.

Regardless, the blue-blooded people of the kingdom of Deucia were quite fond of war. Butcherous, bloody, and baneful it may be, they found it very glorious indeed.

Lord Morales Stools, who preferred to simply be referred to by his family name, was a young man of such nobility, charming, courtly, and proper to the bitter end.

It was perhaps the combination of such opportune characteristics that had led Stools to be named commander in chief of the Deucian army.

Stools would never quite label himself as the type of man to go to war. He was far more the type to stay back in his homeland in the name of defense and climb the rungs of court while the key figures of Deucia were away at war.

Thus, it wasn't a particularly pleasing event when he was summoned to court, only to be informed that he was to part for war at daybreak the next morning.

It wasn't a fully understandable decision, either. To name Stools, who had barely reached his twenty-third year, and had never truly seen war, the commander in chief to the largest army in all the kingdoms, was absolutely preposterous.

He was to later learn that his appointment was a desperate attempt to keep the elite in power, as with the death of the previous commander, there were few capable nobles in the army all together.

As the years passed and battles were fought, Stools proved to be a competent commander. Despite finding war difficult in his initial days, Stools quickly grew partial to the straw cots of the barracks in favor of the plumed mattresses of the palace.

For each battle lost, Stools won two. Year after year, he gained more respect from his men, all the while becoming hardened from his time at war.

Eventually, when Deucia was at a rare period of peace, Stools married a lady of high birth and fathered three healthy children, all raised at court as he was.

All in all, Lord Commander Morales Stools of Deucia was positively typical to the mold his predecessors had left behind.

That was, until the day Stools stood at the head of an army, facing down what was to be the largest battle in history.

The neighboring noble kingdom of Urna had declared war decades ago, and that particular war had been devastating to Deucia. Urna was powerful, and despite the damage the Deucian forces had wreaked upon Urna, they had taken plenty of hits themselves.

Thirty-two years of war led to one day, when both kingdoms called all their men and banners and faced off in the flat sands south of their kingdoms, in a battle to end the never-ending war.

The results would determine not only Stools's life, but the fate of Deucia and its future at war. It was one of the most vital days in history, and any given mishap could shift the tide of the battle.

It was truly unfortunate that Stools had come down with an illness the night preceding the Battle of the Sandlands.

Explosive diarrhea, as it was known in the common tongue, was a painful nuisance of an illness, forcing Stools to visit the loo often in order to avoid an explosive bout of excrement.

It wasn't as though he could postpone the battle, nor could he leave his men without guidance on the field. Stools was truly counting on the perseverance of his bowels and the mutual honor that tied him to Commander Muchen of Urna.

So, Stools found himself sat on his poor stallion, rather hopelessly wishing for the privacy of his loo, wearing extra rags in case of a bowel mishap, and praying to all his Gods that the battle would be swift, unlike his rather explosive state.

By the time the horns had sounded and the armies had begun marching toward each other, Stools already was desperately in need of a loo.

Muchen nodded solemnly across the field at Stools, as their horses trotted toward each other. Dust rose from their chariots, and footsteps of their infantrymen boomed across the field.

Stools, in any other situation, would have lifted his sword and let out a battle cry and led his army charging toward their foes, honoring the silent code that the commanders shared. That wasn't his favored response that day, as he could barely handle the soft trots that his stallion was making that moment.

His face was contorted in obvious discomfort, and Muchen, who had faced Stools on the field plenty, paused in confusion, his hand on his sword as he was ready to respond to Stools's signature war cry. The man cocked his head and turned to his second to discuss what seemed like one of Stools's new battle strategies.

Terron Commode, Stools's second in command, quickly noticed the odd exchange and neared Stools, their stallions barely trotting as both sides prepared to charge.

"Commander," Terron began, "is something wrong?"

Stools let out a strangled noise in response, wincing as his beloved stallion moved underneath him.

"It seems I have not quite recovered from my illness, Terron," Stools strained.

Terron halted his stallion, causing the men behind him to halt as well. He opened his mouth to talk, but Stools had not stopped. Terron followed confusedly, signaling for his men to follow as well.

"No need to worry, Terron," Stools said. "Now sound the cry."

Terron looked hesitant but nodded nonetheless. He turned to his men and lifted his sword. He shook his sword toward the Urnan army and mustered his loudest cry.

"FOR DEUCIA!"

A moment of hesitation from both armies followed, before the Deucians cried back, charging toward the Urnan forces.

Muchen, also after a moment of hesitation, responded and rushed his men to meet the Deucians on the field.

Stools gave a pained cry of his own as he forced his stallion to gallop. The moments that followed were simply torturous.

Stools could see only the trees beyond the Urnan army, where he could see the towers of the nearest fort. His body ached from the strain, and tears gathered in his eyes as he attempted to hold back his urges.

The Urnans neared, but Stools could barely hold himself up, let alone draw his sword to fight. His body begged for relief, and Stools could no longer hold himself back.

He drew his stallion to a screeching halt, screaming all the while. Dust rose up around the Deucian army as his forces followed his lead.

Stools threw himself off his horse, his men slowing in confusion. He was grateful that he had worn black that day, as he knew the fort was simply a backup.

He glanced up from the ground and let out a screech, "*HALT MUCHEN! IF YOU HAVE ANY HONOR, I BESEECH YOU, HALT!*"

Muchen continued to charge. Before he could respond, Stools, on the ground, let out a different breed of a scream. It was a horrifying sound, more so than anything the Urnans had ever heard before.

Muchen screeched to a halt, his knights, his chariots, and his infantrymen halting. Sand rose up around them, and the clear sky was momentarily obscured. As the dust cleared, Stools lay at the head of his army. Silence filled the battleground.

Then, a loud splattering sound emerged. The men behind Stools moved away from their leader, their noses scrunched.

Muchen stared at his second, wondering if this was one of Stools's new battle strategies. Perhaps the Deucian leader had dished out every intelligent thought in his mind to defeat the Urnans once and for all.

The sound continued, and the Urnans stared in puzzlement as men continued to move away. A putrid smell drifted from the Deucian army, and the Urnans paused once more.

Slowly, Stools stood, hunched as though he was carrying the weight of the world on his back. Then, he took a step. And another. And another. Until he was running and the Urnan army braced itself.

As Stools neared Muchen at the front of the

Urnan forces, a revolting odor drifted up from Stools. In the moment that Muchen and his second took to gag and move away, Stools had sprinted between them and continued his seemingly pointless run.

Man after man, the sea of soldiers parted for Stools, all gagging and wincing from the unknown smell. He ran like the wind, pushing aside infantrymen, climbing through chariots, and even crawling under horses.

The Deucian army watched as their brilliant leader created a path. Save for his inner circle, none knew of his illness. To them, Stools was a cunning commander, creating a diversion for the army to attack.

And attack they did.

With dissonant cries, the Deucian army attacked the preoccupied Urnans, charging like the furious sea against ancient coasts.

Turning away was perhaps the biggest mistake the Urnans had ever made, for the tide was then turned against them.

As for Stools, he had then gotten past the initial Urnan forces. The farther back he went, the more confusion that spewed, as none understood the foulness that reeked off the prim commander.

By the time Stools reached the woodlands that

bordered the sands, tears were gushing down his face and chaos reigned behind him. The clashing of metal, the breaking of wheels, and the furious cries of war arose.

But Stools was blind to it all.

He continued to run, until the fortress loomed ahead of him. Joy flooded through him as he sprinted toward the open gate.

The battle was long forgotten as Stools opened door after door, searching for the loo. Finally, there it was: the golden seat of his wildest dreams.

As Deucia prevailed in the distance, Stools, unaware of all else, finally took the coveted seat.

The battle was won.

Home

Khloe Beutler

I am homeless.

Yes, it's true. I dig through garbage cans scavenging for food, clothes, or whatever else I can get my hands on. I sleep on the streets. Sometimes I even sleep on park benches like in the movies, with newspapers for blankets—but only when I'm feeling really brave.

Here are two things about me that you have to know:

1. All I've ever dreamed about was having a mother. My own mother died when I was very young, but I faintly remember little things about her.

2. I'm a child.

The sun pulls me from my slumber this morning. Yesterday, it was crows. The pesky creatures pecked at my hairline, digging their sharp talons carelessly into my skin. It felt like daggers piercing my body.

The amber sunlight is blindingly bright, but I can't complain.

My temple pounds as I sit upright, rubbing the light from my sore, tired eyes. I wonder what kind of day it will be today. Will it be the sort of day blessed by kind strangers? Or will I be faced with the cruel side of the earth? I barely have time to wonder before something heavy crashes into my head with a thud.

I'm thrown backward into the grass, where I rested only minutes ago. The pain in my throbbing head has risen. I reach a finger to the pain source, and upon first glance, I notice I'm bleeding.

"Oh my!"

I hear a voice.

"Oh my, dear!"

It grows louder.

Upon hearing this voice, I feel instantly calm. My heart fills with warmth, and my stomach feels light.

The harsh morning atmosphere has dissolved into something sweeter. Where dogs crazily barked only seconds ago, they've suddenly quieted down. The early morning white noise of the city has been silenced, replaced with a melodic birdsong.

"Oh my goodness, I am so sorry!"

The first thing I notice when I look at this woman is the kind smile plastered upon her cheeks. Two thick, dark eyebrows are tilted upward in concern, as soft pink lips curve slightly. Curly brown ribbons are contained in a low ponytail, while fragments of frizzy locks frame her round face.

I'm sure I've never seen this woman before, but the very sight of her is almost enough to put tears into my eyes. She seems like someone who would love me. She seems like…a *mother*.

"I am so sorry, love."

When her eyes focusing on me, the woman frowns a little. It's nothing I'm not already used to. I like to call it the sympathy face. When people notice I'm a homeless child, I guess they feel pity. To me, it's pretty much all I've ever known.

The second the lady's hand reaches toward me, my spirits instantly lift. A smile tugs at my cheeks, which I'm sure are as pink as the cherry blossoms on her shirt. However, the woman only reaches toward her purse, which must have hit me in the head a couple of minutes ago.

"It…it was an accident. I'm so—so sorry. I have no idea how…gosh. This is…"

Though nothing really has changed, the sound of this woman's calming voice has brought out the sweeter parts of life.

"Hey," I reply, "it's okay."

I hand the woman her purse, and she takes it with a smile. "Well, I better go—"

"Yeah," I interrupt. "You should better get going."

As the woman rises to her feet, I notice a disappointment swelling in my chest. I don't want to accept this feeling, so instead I swallow it deep down and squish a grin onto my cheeks.

"Hey," the lady inquires, "what's your name?"

"August," I reply blandly. "I'm August."

The woman reaches out a hand. Only, this time I know she's offering it to me. I gladly take it and am pulled to my feet.

"The name's Beatrice," the woman beams. "Bea for short. And, August, I couldn't help but notice that you seemed lonely…and I was wondering if you would like to have breakfast with me?"

All of a sudden, the ground begins to sway underneath my feet. My palms fill with sweat, and my knees wobble. I'm certain I just might collapse at any second, but at the same time, I can't contain the smile that bounces upon my cheeks.

"Absolutely!"

There are so many wonderful things about life. Like the way the sun peeks through windowsills during an early summer morning. And diner floors. My eyes like to trace patterns etched into the floorboards.

At the moment, the most wonderful thing about life is pancakes. A big stack of pancakes slathered in syrup and polka-dotted with cinnamon.

I almost can't control the speed in which I shovel large bites of pancake into my mouth. The soft, fluffy substance melts in my mouth as I welcome bite after bite.

The woman giggles a little. Her laugh is softer than clouds made of cotton candy. Every few minutes she takes another sip of her milkshake and glances outside the window.

"You seem to like pancakes a lot," she observes. "Are those good?"

I try to form a weak *yes,* but with a mouth packed with pancake, it's pretty difficult. Instead, an animal-like grunt escapes my vocal cords, and is instantly followed by bits of half-chewed pancake.

Not a second goes by before the woman is sent into an uncontrollable fit of laughter. Soon, we're both giggling uncontrollably in the corner booth at a small diner, with one mouth packed with pancake.

I wish life were always so sweet. I wish the sun always shone this bright, practically blinding my sensitive eyes. I wish I laughed this hard more often, and I wish I could live in this moment, right here forever. Because in this moment, it's just me and her, her and I. I'm here. And I'm safe.

As our laughs simmer out, I notice I'm no longer hungry. My chest has filled with something thick and heavy, and I immediately ask to use the restroom.

"Of course," Bea grins, wiping laughter-induced tears from her eyes. "Go right on ahead."

As I make my way to the bathroom I find I can barely hold myself together. Cold tears begin to leak from my eyes like a drippy faucet. I sniffle my swollen nose, wiping and rubbing my face. My throat burns as I sink to the ground, and burying my face into my arms, I let everything out.

I hear a sound above me.

My heart sinks. It's Beatrice.

At the sight of her, I instantly feel embarrassed. I've only just met her, and I'm already crying in front of her. However, she seems to understand. She crouches down in front of me and her arms outstretch.

When people meet me for the first time, I often notice they never get closer than two feet away from me. Maybe it's because I smell bad. Perhaps it's because they're afraid they might get fleas or parasites or something.

I can't remember the last time I received a hug, but the second Bea's arms wrap around me, I instantly melt.

It feels like a bundle of honeysuckle, dandelions, and lavender. It feels like a warm cup of tea. It feels like music and color, or the smell of the earth after a long-awaited rain. It feels like home.

And suddenly I remember—I remember so well. I remember her hair, the way it always reminded me of coffee. I remember the way she'd stroke my forehead as I drifted off into sleep, and I remember the way her voice, sweeter than birdsong, would wake me in the morning.

My heart fills with a deep ache; a longing far unlike anything I've ever felt before.

"I remember my mother," I confess.

Beatrice pulls away, looking me straight in the eyes. Her soft hand wipes a tear from my face.

"I remember the way she said I love you," I sniffle through scattered breaths. "She always put an emphasis on the word 'you.' It was like a song every time she said it."

A tear slides down Bea's cheek. I chuckle slightly.

"I remember watching the stars with her. We would climb all the way up to the rooftop." My voice trembles and shakes with my breath. "She always made sure I was safe and sound before climbing up after me."

Beatrice pulls me into another warm hug. At this moment, all I can think about is home. After being homeless for as many years as I have, all I have longed for was a home. I've wished for a place I can feel safe and secure. A place where I'll never have to worry about whether or not I belong, because I always will. A place where I can enjoy life—the big moments and the little ones. The things that matter most.

And in this very moment, as I sit with Beatrice outside the bathroom at the small diner, I have a realization. Maybe home isn't a place at all. Maybe the home I've dreamed of after all these years doesn't take place between four walls. Maybe my home…is a *person.*

Beatrice pulls away once again, but this time she rises to her feet. She turns, and for a second, I think she's about to leave. However, she stops in her tracks.

"Come on, kid," her soft, welcoming voice invites, "what do you say we take you home and get you all washed up?"

Home. I've never heard a word so beautiful. Home…

Home…

Home.

The Eagle's Miracle

Camille S. Campbell

Just fourteen hundred more dollars and I can go to auditions at Julliard and pay for my mother's next surgery. I open my sun-stained violin case and hold my dear companion to my chin. Shutting my eyes, I forget where I am. I forget the crime rate of this part of town, the deafening sirens, and the overwhelming smell of crushed cigarettes. I am finally free. The notes glide off the strings, sent off by the bow, all telling a part of a story. I feel as if I'm transported to the vast outdoors, where my ancestors were from. Where they would sing songs near campfires, be one with nature, and roam free with feathers woven in their headdresses, symbols of pride and accomplishment. Their bare feet meet the wet grass, as they listen to the birds singing, the rabbits scurrying through the brush, and the beautiful sound of their own tongue. I forget about hospital bills and how much I need the money. I forget about life itself, because, in this moment, everything's in harmony. I've been playing for hours, not realizing the hazy sky is draining of color.

Chills run up my arm. It's late. Too late. I check

my violin case for money. Forty-five dollars. Better than I thought. Smiling, I slip the cash in my pocket and stride down the road. My shift at Walmart starts soon. I take a seat at the graffiti-covered bus stop, staring down at my shoes.

All of a sudden, a yelp splits the air. I scramble to my feet, realizing that it's the sound of a hurt dog. The whimpers bounce off old building walls and the lids of the garbage cans. Even though my heart races with fear, I take a deep breath and follow the noise. An animal is hurt, and I could never forgive myself for not helping it.

I press my body against the brick wall and calculate my position. Two men in the dark alley loom over a dog; they are like tall pine trees slouching over a wolf cub. The dog is trembling, its brown fur sticking in all directions. Tears shine in its night-black eyes. The creature's left hind leg hangs loosely to the side. They kick the dog to the side, a few feet away from me. Fury rushes through me like a wildfire, and before I know it, I swoop the dog into my arms.

"Hey! Drop *it!*" I hear them say.

Before I can run, one of them grabs my wrist. With a *pop,* he rips the joint out of alignment.

A scream rips my throat.

I kick, trying to pull away, but it's no use. The men

laugh, melting into the shadows, leaving a broken girl and dog behind.

Everything is a blur after that—the ambulance, the hospital. I had agreed to take the dog in once I got better and he got out of the vet. Now, lying on the hospital bed, I gaze down at my cast, but hardly notice it—it's the medical bills I'm concerned about. It's money we don't have. It's dreams that will never come true. I stare at the hospital's painfully white ceiling, trying to ignore the suffocating air that strangles my lungs. I hate hospitals. It's two—maybe three in the morning. I missed my Walmart shift; will I be fired?

I still remember the doctor's words playing in my head. *"What a shame. After this, playing the violin will be nearly impossible."*

I constantly hear sirens wailing outside—more lives shattered. My head begins spinning.

My dreams ruined. My hopes—

I am soon pulled into a deep sleep, away from my reality.

I open my eyes to see rolling green hills, accompanied by clear blue skies. Flocks of birds are swaying through the sky; I can hear water ripple in the distance, along with tribal songs. They sing, "Atvgi'a Ama—Hear the Water" in Cherokee. I automatically sit up, soaking in everything around me. It's beautiful. I look down at the crystal water, admiring the headdress I'm wearing. The feathers, sewn ever so intricately, fill me with pride.

All of a sudden, I see a bird greater than the rest. His golden wings are spread, as he soars through the sky.

"Uwohali," I say in amazement, gazing at the beautiful creature. I've always been drawn to the Native American symbol of freedom and courage. I reach my hand out to the sky, and he swoops down and perches on my forearm. His amber eyes glisten, as he ruffles his feathers.

Don't give up.

I smile, staring into his eyes. My bandaged hand suddenly begins to hurt less. The cast vanishes before my eyes. I am healed. All of a sudden, I hear a violin playing Bach's "Chaconne." I close my eyes, relishing the beautiful notes. I can see my future self at Julliard auditions, playing the violin better than ever. The judges' mouths are open in awe as I breeze through the masterpiece. The piece ends, and the judges begin clapping.

"You have been selected for a full scholarship."

I open my eyes to the same hospital. Now it's dawn. My spirit animal healed me by giving me hope.

Right at this moment, I promise myself that I'm going to fight the battle—to honor my heritage, my mother, my dreams, and myself.

Lilah

Emmy Song

I. Constant

Lilah imagines herself as a porcelain doll, polished and shined just to be displayed. She straightens her red hair so it burns like copper under the sun. She pats away blemishes on her skin like she's erasing mistakes.

Her parents like it better that way, when Lilah is a daughter who can be passed around like a cigarette. Every time her parents' colleagues stare at her with freely roaming eyes, she burns black and blue.

Lilah's father tells her she is too dumb, too ugly, too unwanted to leave this house. As he drunkenly strokes the side of her neck, he says she has to stay with them forever. Her mother, with skin wrinkled like discarded napkins and peeling lips, tells Lilah she's worthless.

Lilah wills her skin into hardened armor, but like spears, their words shatter her defenses. There's no one to put the pieces back together.

II. Linear

She spends her days out in the cornfields, staring at the infinite sky of Wyoming and the shifting clouds. She's jealous of the clouds, free to travel the skies and escape this country town.

Sometimes she thinks of the boy in her English class, whose voice reminds her of the ocean when he reads T.S. Eliot. Or of the undulating lights and foreign chaos of New York City, when he laughs a little too loudly while playing basketball with his friends. He makes her want to live by the water or in the middle of skyscrapers.

Lilah is just another lovestruck teenager with a broken life at home and nowhere to escape.

She wants to be something bigger than herself. Maybe that's why she likes oversize shirts so much, to make her feel larger and more powerful than the girl cowered in the corner who she is at school.

But mostly it's because she pictures wearing his shirts and hoodies, as if their largeness could keep her safe. She wants every day to feel like a fairytale.

III. Quadratic

Summers are the worst. While her classmates vacation in exotic places and drink in the sun's elixir, Lilah is suffocating in townhouses, secrets, and pixels. She decides that she is meant to live a grander life than just this, so she takes her future into her own hands.

Every morning, she encloses herself in a room that reeks of sweet grass and sweat. Her eyes stare at pages of scribbled writing in response to essay prompts and thick textbooks that hold screams and tears in their bindings.

She is obsessed with studying, soaking up formulas and words like the desert after rainfall. Lilah wants to prove her parents and classmates wrong, and show them that she is capable of achieving her dreams on her own.

Lilah finds herself a job cleaning townhouses for rich young families and looking after their children. She's envious of those children, whose future lay uncharted with possibilities that stretch to the skies. The money she earns is not bad, enough to make her hide it in the pages of her chemistry textbook, where she knows her parents won't look.

Her parents are home too often. Most days, they leave Lilah alone while they get drunk and scream at each other, but she is always afraid they will barge into her room and discover her secrets. The days pass by too sluggishly, the humidity clogging her lungs and leaving her choking.

IV. Exponential

September arrives, and with it, senior year. Lilah's classes are all difficult, and the homework keeps her occupied until midnight, when she begins reviewing the next day's lessons in advance. She sleeps for five hours every day, and never has time to visit her field anymore.

Lilah is nervous the first time she raises her hand in class. Her teacher asks what they thought about *Ulysses*, and the other students are reluctant to respond. They sit there, bored, doodling in notebooks and gazing into the distance.

She licks her lips one time, two times, and swallows. Stomach turning, she thrusts her hand in the air, hoping the tremble in her fingers is unnoticeable. From then on, it's easier.

All of a sudden, people are noticing her, including *him*. One autumn day, when the leaves begin to fall burnt orange and gold, he walks up to her and introduces himself as William. The rest of his words are lost on Lilah as she is entranced by the dimples in his cheeks that remind her of the home she never had.

Soon enough, William is Lilah's best friend. He's everything she dreamed of as a six-year-old making up her own Prince Charming. He's handsome, all messy black hair and sparkly blue eyes that dance when he laughs. He treats Lilah like a porcelain doll, a piece of treasure he's afraid to break.

V. Rational

Late in November, Lilah brings him to her field. They lie among the cornstalks and talk about everything, from their childhood and families to their hopes and dreams. When the light begins to fade from the sky, William looks at Lilah and tells her he loves her.

He walks her home, and they are giddy with the excitement of first love. Lilah is wrapped in his basketball jacket, and she thinks that at last, she's living out a fairytale.

They walk up to her house, only to meet her father stepping out of the car. Lilah freezes; she can smell the heady scent of alcohol clinging to her father. He flares up, dragging William to the side, and punches him. Lilah helplessly screams out for him, and her father turns to face her.

He advances on her, a drunken smile warping his face. She tells William to run and leave her behind, and her father hits her in the mouth. Spitting blood, she kicks out and releases the pent-up anger, loneliness, frustration, and fear that built up over the last seventeen years onto her father. The last thing she remembers is curling into someone's arms, as sirens sound in the distance.

VI. Constant

The year flies by like a flock of doves, gently and all at once. Lilah thinks she is glowing today under the sun's golden rays. Her lace white dress hugs her body beneath her navy gown, and her hair hangs loose in its natural curls underneath her cap.

Lilah watches, hand in hand with William, as square hats rain down from the skies streaked with fire. Graduation marks the end of an era, but also the start of a new one. Here, where past falls away and future shoots onward, Lilah can finally feel at peace.

Porcelain (noun):

white clay fired to
high temperatures / tough
and durable / allows light
to shine through

Clear

Resli Ward

Kate didn't remember waking up, but there she was, eyes half-open, staring at the ground. She wasn't quite sure what time it was. All she knew was that she could barely keep her eyes open. Her bed was just next to the window, so when she turned, she could see a single ray of sunshine gleaming through the blinds. She sat up to examine it better and realized the window had a kind of luminescent glow. She wanted to admire its beauty, but a quick glance at the clock told her that she had no time. It was nine forty-eight and her piano lesson was at ten. An oversleep this big was impossible—wasn't it? She began to wonder where the loud noise of the TV was, where the Saturday treat of the smell of cooked bacon was, and most of all where her mother was to get her up, and why she hadn't gotten her up already.

Kate was usually pretty good about getting herself up in the mornings, but today, somehow, she had slept in by two hours.

Oh well, she thought. *I'll just be late or not go.*

She brushed the covers off and stood up, sending a dizzy wave of blood to her head. Kate glanced around her room. Everything was in the right place, but something just seemed…off. She couldn't quite explain what it was, but it made her shiver. She walked out into the hall, which was dark except for natural light. That was the second thing wrong with the morning. Her brothers always left the hall light on, and she yelled at them about it constantly.

"Mom?" Kate shouted. When there was no response, she called again and again, at first confused and then fearing the worst.

Kate liked to personify her anxiety—give it a name so she could explain it better. Time Stealer. Right now, Time Stealer was creeping up on her, looming over her, beginning to control her every move. No matter how hard she tried to resist and tell herself that there was a logical explanation—that she was being crazy—tears pounded in the corners of her eyes, beginning to well up and hurt. Holding too much, her tear glands began to leak, and several drops ran down her face.

"Mom?" she called again, her voice crescendoing until tears were streaming down her face and onto the floor and she was sure the neighbors could hear her.

She walked down the hallway into the living room, tears blurring her vision. No one was there either.

Kate tried to calm down and told herself in a

squeaky voice that they had probably gone to the grocery store or something like that and surely they had left a note somewhere. There was no note at the dining table. Or in the kitchen. There wasn't even any evidence that anyone had been in the house, except, of course, for Kate's wrinkled sheets. The house itself looked brand-new. She felt the tears in her eyes again, pounding.

Trying to calm down, Kate went back to her room and grabbed a tissue. She blew her nose and looked over at her room's single outlet. Last night, her phone had been plugged in and charging, but this morning…whereabouts unknown. This sent Kate into another panic spiral. She took a deep breath, expecting—hoping—calmness would come out.

It didn't. Tears and anxiety came like a waterfall. Kate felt trapped in her own thoughts, like she was drowning in a sea of everything.

That was when she heard knocking at the door. It started out small and meek, growing to the volume of a normal knock. Kate wiped her eyes, took a deep breath, and went to see who it was. The front door was heavy and made a creaking sound as Kate opened it. A girl with a black knee-length dress and a light green sweater was waiting on Kate's porch.

"Oh—uh, hi," Kate mustered.

"Hi," the girl said. "I heard crying and I just came

to see if you're okay. I hope that's not, like, weird."

"No, not at all. Well...a little, but that's okay." Kate wiped a strand of hair from her eyes and sniffled. "I'm fine, thanks for asking."

"Oh, okay. Well, in that case, this is going to be a weird question, but have you seen...well, anybody besides me today?"

"No. Why?"

"I haven't seen anyone either—look outside. There aren't even any cars on the road!"

Kate stepped out into the hot sunlight. Her bare feet felt the dirt in between her toes as she looked out at the road. Not a single car went by.

"Oh my god," Kate said softly.

"Where is everyone?" the other girl asked.

"I don't know."

"I was going to search some of the houses. Do you want to come?"

"Yeah, I guess."

"I'm Kelsey, by the way."

"I'm Kate."

"Hey, K twins!" Kelsey laughed, trying to lighten the mood.

Kelsey was the only one that had the strong suspicion that they were alone, and she didn't like the feeling. A world of silence was an empty space she was afraid she couldn't get out of.

If Kate was honest with herself, she was scared, too. Where was everyone? Where had they all gone?

The two spent the day knocking on doors without any answers. The lights were off in all the houses and other buildings around town. Even the local diner, which was supposed to be open twenty-four hours and was Kate's favorite restaurant, was dark. They approached the Happy Pancake Diner at about two thirty in the afternoon. Kate was trying to take deep breaths to suppress her anxiety. There were no parked cars, no nothing. The door to the building was open so the two went in, Kelsey holding the door for Kate. The smell of breakfast, which was normally ever-present, was absent. The room smelled like nothing.

Kate blinked at the grill behind the counter—she couldn't believe that the entire town was empty. Something stung Kate's head, and she doubled over in pain. Kelsey, who had been looking at one of the booths, came over and put her hands on Kate's shoulders.

"Are you okay?"

"I—I think so," she stammered.

Just then, she heard several voices calling her name. Kate squeezed her eyes shut and tried to drown out the voices. Was she going crazy? Maybe they were just a figment of her anxiety? Thousands of what-ifs clouded her brain, but as quickly as the voices had appeared, they all vanished.

"What happened?" Kelsey supported Kate, and she stood back up.

"I heard all these voices calling my name. It was weird."

"But there isn't anyone else here."

"I know. I guess I'm just hearing things," Kate said.

Kelsey squinted. "Maybe."

They resumed their search.

After concluding that there indeed was no one else in the entire town, they headed back to Kate's house to rest, figuring they needed to stick together. Kate realized that neither of them had eaten all day, nor were they at all hungry. They couldn't find food anyway, so dinner was nothing either.

Just before bed, Kate was washing her face, as she normally did. As she put the damp purple cloth to her face, she began to hear the same voices again. Kate shut her eyes as tightly as she could.

"No! No!" She doubled over in pain. Everything hurt—her stomach, her head, even her toes. She hadn't hurt at all before—what was happening?

Frightened and confused, she realized she was hearing another voice too this time. The voice was deep, probably male. He sounded like he was commanding the situation.

"Get the paddles! Four hundred joules! She's flatlining again! Clear!"

Baby Bluebird

Katie Scala

I met a little girl the other day, who was no more than age six. It was a beautiful Sunday morning. The little girl's smile matched the shining sun outside the hospital's windows. She sat proudly in her chair in the waiting room, and her energy was refreshing to me. There appeared to be no other early birds, for the room was full of silent night owls. So she chirped aloud to herself, her voice like a morning song. She would try to get the attention of the man beside her, but his tired eyes were more focused on the newspaper from a few days ago.

I collected a clipboard and read the name aloud to the quiet room, "Claire Harper?"

The man perked up from his reading and quickly got up from his seat. The little girl jumped up and followed him. Once she caught up with him, she reached for his hand, but he was adjusting his shirt collar.

"Are you the father?" I asked the man as we walked down the hallway.

"Yes," the man answered. "Claire is my wife."

I nodded. "Right this way, sir."

I led the man and little girl down another hallway and stopped outside a door with two chairs outside it. The man turned to the little girl beside him.

"Stay out here," he said before rushing inside the room.

The little girl climbed into a chair. She sat up with her hands in her lap as she happily waited for the man's return, even though it did not seem to be anytime soon. I decided to wait with her so she wouldn't be unsupervised.

"I can't wait to meet my baby brother!" the little girl said to me after a moment. "We're gonna have so much fun!"

"Really?" I asked, standing next to her. "What are you going to do?"

"We're gonna play games!" the little girl exclaimed, kicking her feet up and down. "We're gonna color pictures and play tag together. We can eat ice cream together and play in the park together. I can push him on the swings and go down the slide with him!"

"That does sound fun," I commented enthusiastically. "What other things will you do together?"

“I can help take care of him!” the little girl beamed. “I can feed him and give him his bottle and give Mommy diapers so she can change him. We can also play in the woods behind our house!”

The little girl turned her body toward me, giving me all of her attention.

“When I was really little, I would go into the woods behind my house with Grandpa and we would explore all the trees and flowers. My favorite part was when we looked up and saw the birds. There are so many birds in the forest. Blue birds, red birds, Grandpa even said he saw a yellow bird in the forest once! My favorite bird was a Mommy bird at her nest with little baby birds. Grandpa put me on his shoulders so I could see them—‘but no touch,’ he said! The baby birds didn’t look like the Mommy bird, but Grandpa said one day they will.

“When Grandpa put me down, the Mommy bird came back with a big wormy in her mouth! ‘I’m so happy I don’t have to eat worms,’ I told Grandpa. I’ll make sure my baby brother doesn’t eat worms when we play outside together.”

“When I was little,” I began, “and played outside with my little brother, my mom would always tell him, ‘Birds eat worms. Little boys don’t!’”

“That’s so silly!” The little girl laughed. “I need to remember to tell my baby brother that!”

“Did you go back into the woods with your grandpa?” I said, sitting down beside her.

“Yeah!” The little girl’s smile revealed a tiny gap in her teeth. But then her smile faded. “But later Grandpa said he couldn’t go in the woods with me anymore because he had to stay in his chair. But we came up with a new idea: we watched the stars! They were so bright and sparkly! I tried to count them, but the most I got to was twelve because I lost count. Grandpa would look at the stars with a white sparkle in his eyes, like a tiny star. ‘Is Granny up there in the stars watching us?’ I asked Grandpa. He said, ‘Yes, and I’ll be joining her soon,’ and the white sparkle went down his face. It looked like a shooting star.”

She sighed. “We didn’t watch the stars many times after that. After I went to school for the first time, Mommy said that Grandpa joined Granny in heaven and became a star. After Mommy told me that, I went into the woods by myself, even though I wasn’t allowed to go alone. I was too sad, I told Mommy later. But guess what I found when I was walking?”

“Hmm,” I thought out loud as I noticed her smile back on her face. “What did you find?”

"A baby bird!" the little girl exclaimed, sitting on her knees. "A little baby bluebird! It was on the ground instead of in a nest! I wanted to keep it as a pet, but I didn't know how to take care of it! So I carefully picked it up like this!" She cupped her hands together, forming a tiny bowl.

"I looked for a nest, but the nearest one was too high up! I wanted to give it a worm, but I couldn't find one! So I put the bird carefully in a tree, because there was nothing else I could do. But it will still be my bird, even though I had to leave it. I will always love my baby bluebird.

"When I got home, Mommy was worried about me. I told her I was fine and said I wouldn't go into the woods by myself alone again. But she had good news! She told me that we're going to have a baby, and I'm going to be a big sister! I was so happy! Now I can go in the woods with my baby brother!"

"Your baby brother is like your little bird," I suggested to the little girl.

"But baby brothers can't fly!" The little girl giggled.

"Maybe they can," I told her. "With your help, anything is possible."

The little girl smiled again. Her eyes shone with happiness, like a little bird flying for the first time in a clear blue sky.

Suddenly a doctor opened the door, his eyes distressed and his facial features grim and gray.

The little girl's smile faded. I stood up as the doctor spoke.

"Nurse," the doctor said monotonously. "Please come in. And bring the child as well."

I nodded as the doctor headed back inside the room. I opened my hand as the little girl stood beside me. She took a hold of it, and we entered the room together.

The first thing I heard was muffled sobs. Even with the sun shining strongly through the large windows, the room seemed dark. A woman was sitting hunched over on the hospital bed, head buried in her arms. The sobs echoed from her, bouncing along the walls of the room. Her husband was sitting ice-cold in the chair farthest away from her, his eyes staring into an empty abyss. Two other nurses were also in the room; one was having a quiet discussion with the doctor while the other was going over multiple charts. I could tell they were frantic, but they hid it well enough for the patients not to know.

When the little girl's hand tightened, I realized that she knew something went wrong. I looked over at the bassinette against the wall, where the newborn would lay. But it sat empty.

The doctor cleared his throat, and the mother lifted her head, looking for some good news.

"I'm so sorry," the doctor said, "but the baby didn't make it."

The woman released a loud, ugly sob. The cry was loud enough to break the echo of the hospital's walls. The husband remained still, but seemed to go darker, as if a shadow fell upon him. The doctor bowed his head, then glanced at the nurses beside him; one covered her mouth as the other hung her head in her hands.

I looked down at the little girl, still beside me, still holding my hand. Her brother—her baby brother—was gone. My eyes filled with tears.

Then the little girl, with no smile on her face, yet no tears in her eyes, let go of my hand. With no bounce in her step or sunshine in her smile, she walked up to her mother. The little girl put her arm around her as the woman looked up, her face flooded and ruined.

"It's okay, Mommy," the little girl said. "You did everything you could. There's nothing more you can do. You have to leave him, but he will still be your baby. And you will always love your baby, just like I will always love my baby bird."

Hobbledehoy

Teagan Durkin

Beautiful…

The flickering orange caress of flames on my frozen form.

Terrifying…

This roaring blaze, screeching as it consumes.

Unrecognizable…

Those glints of her teeth as tears trail down to a crazed smile.

Three Hours Earlier

Tick-tock.

Tick-to…

Tiii…

As the clock puttered out, destined for that great timepiece in the sky, a car crawled into the lot. Working a graveyard shift at Peach's Auto Shop and Gas Station—unrecommended for any who enjoy sanity—meant customers were far and few between. And treasured. Filling the tank of a grisly trucker or harried runaway meant a brief respite from this nightmarish job that paid $7.50 an hour, no tips. A break from sticky linoleum floors, creaking pipes I was positive shook asbestos from the ceiling with every groan, and the subtle scent of the owner's roadkill taxidermy fascination leaking out from the break room.

Rousing myself from my drowsiness, I exited the station, squinting against the darkness as I approached the vehicle. The window rolled down, and I leaned in toward the unmoving driver…

And screamed as a putrid cloth was shoved over my mouth.

Five Minutes Later

Campbell's disappointment was evident; her preparations to kidnap me had been thwarted by a lack of readily available chloroform at our local grocer. She was forced to try a lemonade-soaked cloth—"Thought the scent would knock you out," she shrugged—that just reminded me of my grandma's house.

Wonder why I willingly entered the car of someone who had just attempted to kidnap me? An explanation would require hours in order to learn the miles of madness and years of loyalty that was the bond I had with Campbell Torress. Sometimes, though, even I can't fathom how our friendship happened, much less thrived.

We had met in kindergarten, art class, beginning of the year with a teacher who'd be better suited to goat herding or politics. A gaggle of kids had teased Campbell about her painting. She had hugged them.

Dear, peculiar Campbell was a brilliant artist. All set to attend the Rhode Island School of Design once autumn rolled around.

But, that fateful day, Campbell had painted herself.

Literally. She'd smeared dozens of tubes of acrylic paint across her flesh, swirling them like Van Gogh's *Starry Night.*

After Campbell had reduced her peers to tears, and their clothes were ruined, she'd hugged me too, whispering in my ear, "Reality only appears to us tragic because of the disequilibrium and confusion of its appearance. Piet Mondrian."

What else to do besides become friends?

"Hungry?" asked Campbell, yanking me from memory lane.

"Need you ask?" I responded. "What have you got?"

She jerked her head to the back seat, and I turned around to discover Armageddon.

"Cam?"

"Hm?"

"What the bloody devil did you do to your car?" I slightly screeched.

Scattered throughout the back were enough granola bars for a family of five (or Cam for a day), thick rope, canvas, paint jars (some spilling onto the seats), and various items beyond my realm of knowledge.

Eyes still trained on the road, Campbell cracked her spine and said, "Art project. Got to finish one more for my portfolio."

"Dear, Cam, torturer of my mundane soul, riddle me this: How can a you finish your project if it's spilling all over the back seat?"

She sighed. Then she shifted her eyes from the asphalt and abruptly pulled over and stared dead at me with her bloodshot eyes, swirls of brown hair stuck to her sweaty forehead.

"Beloved Quince, light of my life, the dearest friend a madwoman could ask for…this is my art project!"

Cue a blank stare from me.

Realizing I wasn't giving her the desired reaction, Campbell launched into an excited explanation. The truck itself was her final project. She planned to have it represent how highways had become the veins of the Midwest. Somehow there was a connection to kiwi birds and scones.

"And that's how it all ties into the raisins! Get it?"

I nodded, then finally took notice of our location. To the right stood an abandoned house, long claimed by decay, with a forest dominating the landscape behind it. Within that forest resided a wonderland. A clearing, dry and populated by boulders. Close enough that two kids could hike there; isolated enough to feel like freedom.

"You remember," Campbell said as we stood outside the car.

As if I could forget all the hours we had spent there, creating worlds and talking of futures we envisioned for ourselves.

Noting my silence, Campbell gave me a little shove. "Well, come on, moron! Help me carry this."

After grabbing a trash bag, I followed her through the tall grass and thicket, Campbell cursing until we reached the clearing.

"Why are we here?" I asked.

It'd been years since we'd come. The progression of adolescence had pushed this hideout to the back of my mind as tests, love, and college crowded in instead.

Shaking her head and releasing a cascade of curls,

Campbell just gestured me forward. I took tentative steps, and then I halted when I saw it. When I felt it burn my skin.

"Like it?" she queried of the creation before me.

Dug dozens of feet away from the surrounding trees was a monstrous pit and within it a raging fire. Flames within the pit radiated a punishing onslaught of heat, almost brutal to breath in.

"Campbell Torres," I whispered. "What have you done?"

Instead of responding, she reached into the trash bag that'd been dragged from her car. Upturning it, she let loose:

Notes. A dried bouquet of roses. An old sweatshirt covered in paint stains.

Remains of a relationship.

Reminders of my heartbreak.

"Why…?" I asked, my head snapping toward Campbell.

She whispered nothing.

She screamed everything.

Eyes crazed, Campbell started randomly snatching items off the ground, tossing them into the fire as she raged. "Alex left you, Quince, and yet you're still holding on! Threw you out, like you were nothing, like you didn't even matter!"

I watched as everything of the person I'd once loved was thrown into the inferno. Campbell was relentless, feeding the flames until only a single note remained. Scrawled across, in a high schooler's hurried penmanship, were the words, "Love you."

Under Campbell's gaze, I reached down for Alex's love note to me. It had been in third-period English when I'd been passed the note, and I had blushed profusely.

"You were dumped, Quince," Campbell sobbed. "Dumped over text."

A note was all that remained of our relationship.

The main reason for the breakup from Alex was: "We've both got better things coming."

Paper slid between my fingertips as I crumpled the note, tossing it into the fiery behemoth crackling and illuminating the darkening landscape before me. As tears overwhelmed me, I staggered back, and steady arms caught me.

After lowering my shaking body gently to the ground, Campbell hugged me as I cried, and there we stayed until stars painted the inky blue dome above us.

Campbell's smile as the fire raged, teeth pointed

and gleaming, was terrifying. But, just like the fire, it was reassuring. As the flames licked and curled the last memento of the person I'd once loved, I turned toward Campbell. Leaning over, I rested my head upon her shoulder.

And there we stayed, as chaos glimmered before us, two friends absorbed in the flames.

Being a Fangirl Will Save Your Life

Eliana J. Pettigrew

"Good morning!" has to be one of my least favorite expressions—not because I don't like people being cheerful, but because, well, if you're saying "good morning" that means that it's morning time, and that also means that I'm awake in the morning, which isn't a good combination.

Unfortunately, "good morning" was exactly what Christee Fellows said when she stuck her head in my bedroom window at the insane time of six a.m.

"*The Final Tunnel* is being released tomorrow!" was the second thing that she said, which did not improve my mood.

I had heard about the last book in *The Tunnel* series all throughout the last months of school, but I had thought that I would get a break once summer began. Apparently this would not be the case, at least not if Christee had anything to do with it.

"Christee, *what* are you doing in my room at six a.m., and *why* do you think I care about *The Final Tunnel*?" So maybe I was being snappy, but *she* was the one who thought it was a good idea to wake me up for some overrated book.

Don't get me wrong—I love to read. I just don't love to read books that everyone is obsessed with…Books that *aren't even that good*, I might add.

I explain this to Christee as she patiently listens by climbing the rest of the way into my bedroom and walking through the door to the kitchen, heedless of my protests.

"Oh, hello, Christee," my mom says, smiling. "Want a pancake?"

"Mom!" I protest from behind Christee before she can answer my mom. "Don't you think it's a *little* weird that Christee, who didn't spend the night, happens to be in our kitchen? Don't you want to know why she's here?"

My mom tips her head to the side. "Well, obviously she's here because of the new book—"

"*You* know about that?"

"Well, of course! The author is actually one of my favorites."

"I don't believe this!" I groan, plopping into a chair. "You didn't know what an emoji was, but you know about some random book series?"

"It's not random!" protests Christee, piling her plate with pancakes. "There are more than—"

"'Two hundred million copies printed,' I *know*," I

finish. "It's ridiculous."

Christee and my mom exchange a look. "Well, maybe you'll change your mind," says Christee.

"I shall not!" I declare. "Why would I change my mind?"

"I just think that after you spend some time devoted to the fandom—"

"What? What time? What are you talking about?"

"We're going to camp outside the library, remember?"

"Umm, no? I *don't* remember because you never *told* me." I look from my mom to Christee, and *oh no.* Both of them have that "it's already decided" look on their faces. I begin to shake my head vigorously, but I know it's futile.

"Isn't this *fun*?" Christee says in a voice that tells me she knows I'm thinking the opposite. We're smooshed into a little tent, waiting outside of the library.

"Why couldn't we wait outside the bookstore?"

"The bookstore is so *expensive.* And besides, an inside source tells me the library will be purchasing the book tomorrow as well."

I roll my eyes—both of us know Christee's "inside source" is her cousin, James, who shelves books on weekends.

"Besides, there's no one else here, which means we get a prime spot."

"No," I correct her. "There's no one else here because no one in their right mind would be crazy enough to wait outside a *library* for a book release. At least the bookstore's having a release party tomorrow."

"Tomorrow it'll be too late!" cries Christee dramatically. "By Sunday evening all the speed-readers will be spoiling the ending!"

I'm about to point out that she can avoid people spoiling it for her if she just stays offline until she's done with the book when a thought occurs to me.

"Christee, what did you say?"

"I said by tomorrow afternoon everyone will have finished the book—"

"Christee, the library's *closed* on Sundays!"

Christee looks at me like I've grown a third head. Her hand flies to her mouth.

"Oh my gosh, you're *right*!" she exclaims. "What do we do?"

I'm already unzipping the tent. "We go home, go

to bed, and forget this happened."

Christee follows me through the tent flap.

"Maybe we can still go to the bookstore—" she's saying when suddenly she gasps and I follow her gaze up the street.

A streetlight makes the silhouette of the woman under it seem dark and mysterious.

"Chill, Chris, it's just someone walk—" I start to say, but Christee has recovered from her shock and is sprinting down the street.

"What are you doing?" I shout after her, and she looks over her shoulder at me, not even slowing down.

"I'd know that outline anywhere!" she says triumphantly.

Not knowing what else to do, I run to catch her.

"Tara! Tara!" Christee is screaming and waving her arms. Literally *waving her arms.* The stranger under the streetlight has somehow not seen us yet, and Christee engulfs her in a hug from behind.

"*What* are you doing?" I exclaim as the stranger flails her arms.

"You're the actor for Tara from *The Tunnel: Year One*! I can't believe you're here!"

"I'm the—who?" The battered-looking brunette looks as confused as I am.

"Wait, or are you just a really good cosplayer?"

Christee doesn't notice the confusion around her. "Can I take a picture?" she asks, scooting even closer to the confused woman. She reaches into her pocket to grab her phone. The movement accidentally knocks the stranger's bag to the ground.

"Oops, sorry!" says Christee, scurrying to pick up the strewn contents.

I put a hand on Christee's shoulder to tell her to chill as she grabs a mysterious shining object from the ground where it has fallen from the purse.

"Don't!" is the last thing we hear, a warning that comes too late.

"Where are we?" I'm panicking. Dirty walls curve into a ceiling around us, and I don't see an exit. Behind us is a wall; in front is a continuation of the tunnel.

"This is…we're in *The Tunnel*!"

"Okay, seeing that actress has clearly gotten to you," I say. "You just stay by me, and I'll ask someone for directions." I start to walk away when an eerie sound cuts through the air.

"Um, what's that?" I ask, nearly backing into an excited Christee.

"That's the bell! That's the bell!" she cheers.

"Aaand...what does *that* mean?" I decide to follow whatever game Christee's playing.

"That means—that means we have to *run*!"

Suddenly my arm is being yanked out of its socket as Christee takes off. I don't have any choice but to follow her, unless I want to be short a limb, and for the second time tonight, I'm running after Christee.

"Why—are—we—running?" I pant. Christee is insanely fast.

"This is part of the First Tunnel, I think." She doesn't even sound winded. She's actually *enjoying herself.* "We have to make it to the Seventh Pool—that's where the crystal is hidden."

"Crystal? What pool?"

Christee shakes her head. "It's explained in the fifteenth chapter—the crystal is where you can wish—within reason—for something."

Chapter? This is insane. She's talking about a book. I'm about to skid to a halt when I hear a ferocious noise behind me.

"What is that?" I ask, just as Christee yells "Don't stop!" and pulls me into a wide crevice. I look at the spot where we were just running as a giant tennis ball rolls past. The neon monstrosity is bigger than my entire house.

"Okay, so maybe this isn't made up," I whisper.

"You *think*?" Christee frowns at me. "Good thing I read that scene sixteen times—otherwise we'd be tennis ball mush." She starts to crawl out of the crevice, but I grab her sleeve.

"What are you doing? You can't go out there! What if it's a giant bowling ball next?"

Chrsitee shakes her head, incredibly calm. "There's no more sports equipment until at least chapter thirty. Besides, we can't stay here—the tunnel floods."

"*Floods*?"

I hear Christee shouting for me to wait, because now I'm way ahead of her.

My side is on fire and my legs feel heavy when Christee puts an arm out. "This is it."

We're in front of what looks like another giant crevice. I can hear water past the opening. We've run past a mammoth soccer ball, a gondola-size skate, and even some ill-intentioned circular cereal. As I take heaving breaths, she reminds me: "Be glad I read the books—we avoided all the things Tara had to deal with."

What happens next is blurry. Climbing into the crevice, Christee touching a huge crystal and grabbing my hand, and warm, engulfing light.

"Girls?" My eyes open to take in the face of James, Christee's cousin. "Can I, um, help you?"

We're outside the library, lying on the grass strip. I'm not sure how to explain this. Before I can accidentally blurt out our adventure, Christee jumps in.

"You see, we were going to camp here—I forgot the library's closed tomorrow—and then I said, 'Wouldn't it be cool if we slept on the lawn?'"

James is looking skeptical already—but then Christee starts spouting randomness about *The Tunnel* and how she thinks sleeping on the lawn is parallel to it, and James stops listening.

"Fine—I'll take you home."

At my house, Christee whips out *The Tunnel: Year One*—"I never leave home without it!"—and demands I start reading. "You know you want to."

Rolling my eyes, I open the paperback. "Fine, but

only so I can figure out why giant objects are in a tunnel."

Look Up

Emily Sun

A balloon is stuck in a green canopy.

It's lodged in a cluster of leaves on the highest branch of the tallest tree in this park. Squint, and you will see it's one of those foil balloons yelling "Happy Birthday!" in bouncy script and colors.

Today, rain pours out of the empty sky and batters the shine, and a little bit of helium, out of the balloon.

Two months ago, the balloon was printed and cut by a tired machine in Kansas. The fourth global helium shortage had skyrocketed helium prices, which turned a floating balloon into a $135 luxury.

Two workers, clad in blue-gray uniforms, stood at the end of the assembly line with stiff knees. Their hands swiveled between collecting the finished balloons and folding them into cardboard boxes.

"Doesn't it bother you?" a worker with black roots peeking through their dyed red hair yelled above the high-pitched whir of the machine.

"The noise? No, I'm used to it by now." The other worker shrugged and flicked their head back, forgetting for a moment they had buzzed off their hair.

"No, that people are dropping half a week's worth of our salary on one balloon. Or that companies are hoarding helium for party supplies when there's barely enough for the important stuff."

"Like?"

"MRI machines. Cleaning rockets' fuel tanks. Making phones. Did you see that photo of a baby turtle suffocated by a balloon string?"

The buzz-cut worker shook their head, trying to shake the glare of the reflective foil balloons out of their eyes. The red-haired worker took that as a no and sighed.

The only sound in the factory room was the screeching of machine gears turning and the crinkling of balloons. The buzz-cut worker tried to ignore the crick in their neck that was starting to form from looking down for too long. The red-haired worker tried to sever the connection between their hands from their mind as if they could convince themselves it was someone else assembling these potential murder weapons.

"I can't stand this." The red-haired worker groaned.

"Calm down. There are only five minutes before we can go home."

"No, I can't stand *this*." The red-haired worker slapped their hands on the conveyor belt and stalked toward the exit. "I'm going to hand in my resignation letter."

The buzz-cut worker switched off the machine. They spoke to the shadow of their coworker. "I'll see you tomorrow."

Two weeks ago, the balloon hid inside an untouched pink gift box. The box sat in the middle of a glass coffee table. A sixteen-year-old hugged her knees on a velvet sofa and glared at it through thick blue eyeliner. Her dad leaned toward her from a tufted ottoman, his button-down shirt pressed to perfection.

"You didn't have to get me anything."

"I know."

"I asked you not to."

"Just open it."

The girl glared at the box, then her dad, then reached out one finger to flick the lid open. The balloon rose up, the "Happy Birthday!" gleamed from the light of the setting sun, and it bumped into the crystal chandelier that hung overhead.

"A balloon?" She watched the balloon bounce then come to rest on the ceiling.

"A floating one."

"I'll hang it on the balcony." The girl stood up and snatched the string of the balloon. She watched the city below her. Her voice hardened, and she pelted her words at her dad. "That's what you want, isn't it? For the world to see how rich you are that you can waste money on crap like this?"

"What? No!"

The daughter flinched at her dad's voice coming from behind her, and the balloon slipped from her grasp.

"Dammit."

The two watched as the balloon blew into a nearby park and disappeared behind the foliage.

"It's fine."

The girl stomped back to the couch and flopped down, closing her eyes. "I'm not sorry to you. I'm sorry to the poor bird that's gonna kill."

The dad followed on silent footsteps, sitting next to her feet. "Remember how we'd buy balloons by the bunch back when you were a kid and helium wasn't so expensive?" His daughter pressed her cheek into the scratchy velvet. "It was never enough to lift you off the ground, but you were obsessed with flying and seeing what's 'up there.'"

The silence stretched for miles until it was cut off by a quiet voice. "Thanks."

Two years from now, a turtle will lie on a metal operating table. A pair of gloved hands will slice through the underside of its shell with a scalpel. Its head will fall from left to right as the hands dig through the turtle's insides, blue gloves staining red in search for a cause of death. It will be this intern's first necropsy at the marine laboratory, and they won't be able to straighten out the tremor in their breath or blink the tears from their eyes when they cut open the turtle's intestines.

"Green sea turtle. Found dead on a beach. Cause of death: starvation and dehydration from plastic ingestion."

The intern will pick through the flesh with a pair of tweezers and drop piece after piece into a tray.

"Rubber bands, plastic bags, and ..."

The last piece of trash will catch the fluorescent light and the intern's eyes. It is bigger than the rest, and when the intern smooths it out, they will see the faint outlines of an H, two P's, and a B.

"And a birthday balloon."

Evergreen

Arria Haigler

Georgio was only about five when Mama left us.

See, the plants got bad a long time ago. Whatever the farmers were putting in them made them go a little wild. And by "a little wild," I mean you've gotta sleep with a knife now, so in the morning, when the vines and such have grown over your body, you can cut your way out.

And that sucks a ton, but Georgio makes the best of it. He's always telling me, "Well, at least we've got somethin' to eat. It could be like a zombie movie, where you can't even have a burger, 'cause it'll bite ya back!"

Whenever he says stuff like that, I just rustle his hair and hope he doesn't ever stop sayin' stuff like that.

Nowadays, I've always gotta be the one to say stuff like, "Now, Lil' Gio, if you insist on only eatin' from outside, at least make sure the berries aren't on a poison ivy bush this time!"

"Don't call me little!" Georgio's always callin' back, scratchin' his fat, red cheeks like the Devil's got on 'em.

I guess he's not so small now. He's about seven, and a couple of nights ago, he cut himself out of a pea plant. Still, about seven is young enough to be my Lil' Gio.

Well—in all honesty, I don't even know if Georgio's seven. I'm not sure I even trust the calendars or the clocks to tell me when it is anymore. Ever since Mama left, I'd only trust the sun itself to tell me the time of day.

But that option's long gone. The trees and shrubs grew over a long time ago. They had the best and brightest working on it, and some of us normal people, too. They were trying to kill 'em with all kinds of "icides," herbicides included, even though we figured out a while back that just made 'em stronger. They tried burning 'em, and cutting 'em, and drownin' 'em, until eventually they all gave up. One day, the sun got a lot hotter than it had ever been, and the trees started growin' taller than they had ever gotten—and then the sun just stopped hitting the ground. It's darker than a country house with the lights out all day long now, and we all just had to learn to be fine with that.

Back before Mama left, and we used to see a drop of sunlight hit the ground, she would tell Georgio and

I to go stand in it. Said we needed our vitamins.

Gio'd always knock me over when we did. Gio had what I liked to call "Break Ankle Syndrome." He'd had it ever since we were teeny. Every time he was given some task, whether it be just standin' in the sunlight, or feedin' Earnie the Turtle for his first-grade class, he had a tendency to trip over his own foot. Not only did he knock over Earnie's tank, sending him to his early demise at forty-three, but he sprained his ankle every time we played tag.

Now taking care of him is up to me. Mama said she was going up north, said they'd got some kinda elixir whipped up better than what we had down here to fix this whole mess. She'd heard about it on the TV, said it wouldn't take long for her to get hold of it and come back. Said when we woke up in the morning and the sun hit our faces, for the first time in a long time, she'd be back there with us. And she wasn't ever gonna leave us, not ever again.

I haven't lost hope. I'm hopeful. Gio's hopeful. And I trust Mama—I do—but we couldn't wait for her any longer. When she left, every day I'd get up in the morning, and I'd put my shirt over my face, cause Mama said too much air is dangerous just like none, and I'd flick on the big ol' flashlight she'd bought me for Christmas, and point it out into the woods.

And I'd sit.

And I'd wait.

And at a certain point in the evenin', Gio would ask me for dinner. He'd already have the can of tuna. He just wanted me to acknowledge him and give him the "Sure, have at it" before he ate it. Until one day there was no more tuna.

And it was just me and Gio.

In the cold, dark house.

On the cold, dark porch.

Nothing but us and whatever was out there. And nothin' to do but leave.

Georgio was about six when we left the house.

And we haven't been back since. Not that we'd know how to. I tried to teach Gio left from right once. And now he thinks north and up are the same. Not that it matters much. It just irritates me.

"Let me hold the compass. You taught me how to do it!" he called to me once.

I didn't even indulge him.

When we left the house, I found three handheld flashlights Dad used to keep in the garage. I strapped a flashlight to Gio's left arm and another to his right leg so he could see where he was goin'. Then I got the reflectors off every bike in the house and taped them to either side of him, so I could see where he was going. I strapped the third flashlight to my left leg, and I carried the big one around. I was lookin' for him to be ahead of me, and then—

Thwamp! He stomped on a mushroom bigger than our two heads put together behind me and scared the hoppin' heebie-jeebies outta me.

I sighed and kept walkin'. He was pokin' fun at me.

"You know why I can't hold the compass?" I told him. "'Cause little boys with nappy afros who get their black from not bathin' don't get to hold the compass."

"I get my black from my mama, just like you, Leo!" Gio tugged on my unraveling braid. He added after a moment of uncharacteristic silence, "And *she'd* let me hold the compass."

I squeezed the compass to my chest. I knew it was a guilt trip. I'd lived alone with Gio for two years. When we still lived at the house, he guilted me every night into lettin' him eat my old chocolate puddin'. He really didn't need to. I wasn't gonna eat three-year-old freezer-burned puddin'. He just enjoyed the sport of beggin', so I'd let him think he had pulled one over on me.

But this—this was important.

We couldn't lose the compass. For a year we'd been following it, and if I didn't have it to trust, Gio couldn't trust me. I held it so tight I could feel my mother's first and last initials carved into it.

I closed my eyes and sighed louder then I ever had before. "You know what," I began, and I heard Gio turn to me. "Just…be careful. You're not gonna fall over. You're not gonna break your ankles. You're just gonna hold it and tell us which way is north. Okay? You've got it. You're gonna do great."

I handed it to him, and as he turned, I reached my hand out to squeeze his shoulder, but I didn't feel him. I tried again, this time flailing a bit more to try and snag him.

"Gio?" I called out for him.

No response.

I raised my voice, a hair higher than usual. "Gio?" My voice cracked. "Gio, this—this ain't funny."

I waited, tried to calm my breathing, tried to stop all the nasty things running through my mind. It was so silent I could hear my lips part as I shivered. I took in a raspy breath, and a tear fell down my cheek.

I closed my eyes.

Hugged my flashlight to my chest.

And screamed out Gio's name with all I had.

I woke up at the bottom of a long hill. All around me was darkness, and I couldn't hear Leo.

"Leo?" I whispered.

No one called back.

I jumped up, brushed off my pants, and tried to get the guck off me. "Leo!" I called. "I didn't lose the compass. I've got it right here!" I whisper-hissed at him.

I swatted at the flashlight strapped to my arm. It flickered but didn't light. I stomped, and the one on my leg did. I hopped around, using the light to look for the compass.

I fell on a vine next to me.

And I found this split between the trees. And what an unfamiliar thing I saw there.

There was this space, and there was only grass on the ground. Just grass. And all over the grass, a light shone down from the sky and warmed my face.

And I started to cry. I felt like Leo. He's always ballin' for one reason or another, but this was for a reason. Across the clearing, there was a tree. And on that tree, there was a dress. And I knew that dress.

It couldn't be anyone else's.

My daddy sowed it for my mama outta my blue baby blanket.

I walked across the clearing, and I draped my arm across the dress. And I sobbed.

The People You Leave Behind

Thea Tinker-Avitabile

The day before, Eli had told Colin that she wanted to start the summer off right. Now she was sitting in a full bathtub with all of her clothes on, tears silently dripping from mascara-stained eyes.

She didn't want to think. Facing what she was feeling was too hard.

She tried to suppress her thoughts by letting her head sink underwater, but that only made it easier to think. The water closing in on all sides got rid of all other noise, leaving her mind at full volume. She covered her ears as if that could silence it, but it didn't distract from the hollowness she was feeling.

After a minute, she lifted her head out of the water, gasping for air as she grasped the sides of the bathtub. The water ran down her cheeks, mixed with the tears and snot still flowing from her eyes and nose. Her long jet-black hair rested atop the water, floating and splaying out in front of her. It looked like a picture you would find in an edgy modern photographer's portfolio, depressing and lonely, yet beautiful.

She stared up at the tiled ceiling, her neck aching

from the position she had been sitting in.

A knock sounded on the locked door, echoing throughout the bathroom. Eli jumped, causing water to splash out of the tub and onto the furry white rug next to her.

"Eli? Is that you in there?" Her mom's muffled voice sounded concerned, and Eli could see the door handle jiggling.

"Yeah, it's me," she said, slowly pulling herself out of the bathtub, making sure no water spilled over.

"Can I come in?"

"Uh, not right now, Mom, I'm kinda busy,"

"Are you sure you're okay though, honey?"

Eli leaned against the door, her head resting against the solid white wood. She didn't answer.

"You knew that boy, didn't you?"

Eli laughed. Laughing made the world seem a little less crazy and out of proportion.

"Colin's in the living room if you want to see him." Her mom waited for a few seconds before Eli could hear her footsteps walking away, leaving her alone, sitting against the door.

She stood up, reaching for the door handle and letting her hand rest on it for a while. *One who hesitates is lost.* She was already so lost, yet some outer force compelled her to turn the doorknob. She stepped outside of the bathroom, the carpet beneath her feet feeling so alien even though she had felt it every day of her life. Her wet clothes stuck to her figure as she walked down the hallway. The footprints she left behind her were wet and sloppy, trailing around and around. She reached the staircase and stood at the top of it. Colin was waiting for her on the couch, ready to comfort her, ready to tell her that it wasn't her fault and that the whole drive-in thing was in the past. He was going to tell her he was there for her if she needed anything. He was going to tell her that it wasn't her fault Justin had gotten into that ca—

Yet when she sat next to him on the couch he didn't say anything.

"I don't want to go back to school," she said, her hair leaving a wet place on the pillow behind her.

"I know." Colin wrapped his arm around her, ignoring how wet she was.

They sat there for what seemed like hours, saying nothing. At some point Eli had started crying and so had Colin. The small orange couch held their crying bodies as they leaned into each other. He did not come to her house to see if she was okay. He already knew she wasn't. Colin had come to grieve with her.

He had come to cry with her.

Eli's mom walked into the room, and Colin stood up abruptly, wiping the tears from his eyes.

"Me and Eli are leaving this house." He said it like nothing could change his mind. It was final.

He grabbed her hand and stared her mom straight in the eye, but she just nodded, a tired and happy smile on her face as if she had been waiting for her child to move on.

Colin looked shocked for a second, but he recovered and pulled Eli off the couch, stomping all the way to his red Mercedes-Benz that was parked outside of her house.

The wind blew through her hair as they sailed down the streets of Sacramento, the ugliness of the city striking her hard across the face. Everywhere she looked she saw something that reminded her of him. The corner store they used to visit every day after school, the tree they sat under when she tried to get him out of one of his moods, the weak chain-link fence they scaled to get to Rayview, the alley they smoked in with his annoying friends, and…the drive-in.

"Stop here," she said quietly, and Colin looked over at her, then at where they were.

"Eli…" He looked at her with a pained look in

his eyes. "Do you really want to do this to yourself?"

Eli didn't answer. She just stepped out of the car and headed for the ticket booth. She could hear Colin get out behind her, and she slowed, waiting for him to catch up.

They stepped into the deserted lot, and the only sound they could hear was the birds and their shoes slapping against the pavement. It was summer, yet the sky was a smoky gray and the clouds were full. The giant screen was blank, a perfect white, the brightest thing in a mile's radius.

Eli could feel Colin behind her, and she turned. He was crying.

"I…I saw him here, y'know."

He said it out of thin air, his lips barely forming the sentence. She could see his arms shaking, and anger flowed through her veins, her shoes now pounding against the pavement until she came barreling into Colin, knocking him to the ground. She heard his head hit the ground hard, but she didn't stop. She could feel her knuckles crack as they hit his face. Her fists went down on him again and again, and she couldn't stop and she was so scared and so sad and so angry and she just wanted Justin back. She wanted to see him again. She wanted to talk to him one more time. One more dumb conversation about whether his favorite movie should've won an Oscar or not.

She stayed there, crumpled on top of Colin's semiconscious body until she decided she could speak.

"Why didn't you stop him?" Her words came out raspy and broken.

Colin didn't answer.

"Why didn't you stop him!" she yelled, her voice attracting unwanted attention from people walking down the street. She didn't care.

"There's no way I possibly could have kno—" he said, his face crumpled in pain.

"Why didn't you stop him?" Eli repeated, her mind full of the perfect white-hot anger of the drive-in screen.

"You can't predict a car cra—"

"Why didn't you stop him?" She could see the blood flowing from his nose and wiped it away.

"Eli..." Pain was laced into his voice, and she could tell it wasn't from his injuries.

"Why didn't you stop him?"

"I don't know."

Colin stood up weakly, his legs threatening to

buckle under his limp body. He pulled Eli up with what little strength he had and then turned away from her, his arms wide.

"I DON'T KNOW!" he yelled into the abandoned lot.

It came right back to him, echoing all around the drive-in. A chill swept through Eli, and she stepped closer to Colin, pulling him into a tight embrace.

"It's not your fault, Colin. I'm sorry. I didn't—"

"I know."

"I don't think you do."

Colin's red Mercedes-Benz sailed down the streets of Sacramento once again, its tires screeching against the paved and potholed roads. Eli's surroundings still seemed ugly and still brought back terrible memories that were once beautiful and happy. Still, she felt something near closure, although she wasn't exactly sure what that word meant, for she had no clue how someone could ever get over someone they loved.

Eli closed her eyes, and Justin was still sitting in the back of the car, smoking a cigarette with his feet propped up on the back of her seat. He and Colin were having a heated argument over what sports team was better while she just smiled and looked back at his smiling face. Colin had sunglasses on, but she could tell his eyes were on the road. He was smiling, something she hadn't seen since Justin had…died. The three of them were the only people in the world that existed in that moment. Young and carefree and together. There was no future or past. There was no fear or guilt or anger or sadness. Only peace.

Wings

Rachel Berger

It all began at the little house on the hill. Frigid wind howled loudly, sending the rusted weathervane into frenzy. The worn-down mailbox swayed, dangerously close to falling over. Blue paint peeled off the discolored gates, stained gray from the pounding rain.

I struggled to find a cause for my sadness as I cried. This is what I had wanted: a life in the shadows. To be ignored consistently, thrown to the side like an old piece of jewelry that nobody wanted. To simply be left alone.

But no matter what happened, I was always able to find an empty space in my heart… My mind held me captive in a dark pool of sorrow, and I was slipping to the deep end.

Time seemed to pass impossibly down tempo. Each *tick* of the clock was drawn out sluggishly, slower than cold molasses. I spent what must have been eternities in solitude. I remained locked within the cage that was my own mind.

As the minutes dragged on, I fell deeper and deeper into the abyss of my mind. There was a difference this time. I was falling peacefully. The descent was not one of sadness, either. Colors swirled around me, royal blues and deep purples replacing the dull gray I was used to. I marveled at the supernatural beauty of how the colors danced, mixing and creating a lovely pigment I could not name. I knew what was happening. My mind was trying to give me some peace, but I was so lost in my own body…

My melancholy made me quite oblivious to what was happening outside. The storm was raging. Trees bent in the gale, some even breaking in half and falling. My little house was starting to shake violently, in perfect tempo with the angry tempest.

I was roughly pulled back into reality when the sensation of falling filled me. My eyes snapped open and searched, hunting and failing to find the cause. It was when I sat up that it hit me. My house was plummeting, taken by a terrible storm-induced mudslide.

I knew I was cascading to my death, that I would never set foot on the earth again, but I felt unexplainably buoyant. My miserable life would be over at last. I would meet my end quickly, and then there would be nothing. I was ready, but the universe had something else in store for me.

An odd burning sensation erupted on my back, slowly increasing in temperature. It was painful enough that I was distracted from my sudden burst of happiness. I touched my icy hand to my skin in hopes to soothe the burning fire. When I felt two small bumps forming, I sighed. My death wouldn't be as peaceful as I had imagined. I would die from some dreadful illness…

The fire got impossibly hotter, and my vision blurred. I knew this would be the end. I closed my eyes…

And I was flying.

I looked down at my house as it plummeted into the depths of the storm while I climbed higher and higher in the sky. I felt my back again in awe, incredibly confused. In the place of the scorching fire was a pair of *wings*. I craned my neck to get a better look at them. My wings were pearly white and felt smoother than silk.

I soared high above humanity, gazing in wonder at what I saw. Birds flew under me, creating beautiful patterns and formations. Clouds lazily drifted around me. The sun shone brightly, illuminating the entire scene.

In that moment, all of my worries disappeared. I was truly and utterly happy, bursts of laughter escaping in uneven lurches from my lips. The dark, metal cords that tied me to my depression were swiftly cut, replaced with colorful bands to hold me to this

new way of life.
I was free.

Reflections

Rhea Bajwa

Jamal grunted as he brushed aside rubble, his back aching and creaking as he lifted yet another piece. He reflected on the honor of being a slave for Queen Snow White.

Wait, what was that? With new vigor, he hurled away loose wreckage to come upon a shattered mirror. He scoffed and turned away, when a frail voice stopped him. "Wait!"

He spun around in shock, eyes roving the room looking at the other slaves, but no one paid any attention to him. *Where did that voice come from?* He peered down cautiously at the mirror and then shook his head.

"Down here, yes, over here!" The voice was hoarse, and yet shrill in his ears. It came undoubtedly from the mirror.

He knelt and swooped up one of the fragments of glass. There it was: a glimpse of a…a man. Skin as pale as ivory, and hair a flaxen weave. Only his face was visible.

He whispered, "Please, listen to me! I was just like you."

Jamal cut him off. "Who are you? How are you in a mirror?"

Wait, was this the evil mirror that helped the wicked queen attempt to kill Snow White? This was dark, dark magic.

"You monstrosity!" he growled.

"No! Listen to me!" the mirror pleaded, but Jamal had already picked up his ax.

"I will crush you!" Jamal screamed.

The man in the mirror winced and muttered, "It doesn't matter. I don't have much longer anyway."

"Any last words?" Jamal snarled.

"Yes, let me tell you a story! It's my last wish!"

Jamal was now intrigued. The man's exhausted appearance made Jamal pause. It seemed a year of his life was peeling off him every minute. Jamal hurriedly shook his head as if to rid any pitying thoughts. This was the villain who had tried to kill his queen. However, he wasn't heartless and listened as the man in the mirror spoke.

The day was crisp and tart. Thin threads of cloud hovered over the sky, and there was a breeze weaving through the air.

"Hurry up, you piece of dirt!" the guard ordered William, one of the many slaves walking to the castle.

William gritted his teeth and cast his eyes low, mumbling a mundane response. His tanned hands gripped the edge of his shirt. His anger rose as he took his first step into the glittering castle.

It was magnificent—tall columns of crystal colored the purest shades of dark purple and blue, with a sprinkling of diamonds in the ceiling. Standing there felt like being nestled against the sky's very breast.

A sharp shove sent him sprawling back to reality.

"Move it. We ain't paying you for standing around gawking," a palace guard snapped.

"We ain't paying them regardless, Jerry," another guard said. Then they roared in laughter.

That was when she entered. The most beautiful woman William had ever seen in his life. He stared awestruck at her. He wasn't even sure if he could call her a woman. She looked like a deity. She was ethereal. An obsidian gown was wrapped around her tall figure. Her lush hair was swept to one side. Her oval-shaped mouth opened, but William didn't hear a word she said.

All through the day, William's mind lingered on her. He yearned to know more about her—what was her favorite delicacy, her favorite animal, anything.

Only two weeks after his arrival, he was summoned by the queen herself. In vain he tried to smooth back his unruly hair and hurried to the queen's chambers. His heart thumped nervously as he was ushered in, and there she was again, alone. Wearing nothing but a thin gown. Even dressed this simply, she looked gorgeous.

"William Morein," she said.

Hearing his worthless name from her lips seemed to give it so much more importance. It sounded so right coming from her.

"I am Anastasia," she said, introducing herself.

She asked him about his interests, and they spent hours talking. When he left the chambers, William was delirious with happiness. But he was a bit apprehensive. After all, she was married to the king. However, he brushed those thoughts away, to his own peril.

They started meeting much more frequently, and a month passed before he knew it. William and the queen, who he now knew as Ana, got closer and closer.

One day, they both were lounging in Ana's chambers when she suddenly kissed him. He froze in shock.

"I am in love with you," she whispered in his ear. "And I need you to kill the king. If you love me, you will do it."

Her words made William's blood run cold, and he pulled away and asked her if she was crazy.

However, sweet Ana's soft cajoling eventually convinced him to do it.

That night William snuck into the king's chambers and killed him. He held a pillow to his head and sobbed quietly, knowing he was committing a heinous crime. He knew what he did that night would never leave him. He tried to justify that he was doing this for the woman he loved, but he couldn't shake the sensation that this was all too sudden, and no one said "I love you" after a month and then asked them to kill their husband.

He blocked these thoughts and quietly stepped into Ana's room, shaking after what he had done.

Ana turned around, and hearing the horrific deed was done, she suddenly burst out laughing.

"It's done?" she asked.

He nodded.

"Thank god, I was getting sick of saying how much I love you!"

What was Ana saying?

"I'm sorry?" William stuttered.

What was Ana saying? How could she say that?

"But I—I thought—I—"

She cut him off, cackling. "You thought what? That I care for you? That I actually love you? My dear, I simply gave your pathetic life a purpose!"

"What? It's impossible! Please I…I love you! Don't do this to me."

He dropped to his knees, shaking his head in disbelief.

She sashayed to her full-length mirror, ignoring him, smoothing down her hair.

"Darling, don't beg. It's pathetic," she scolded him, smirking.

"You…you promised me we would be together forever!" William screamed out in desperation in a last attempt to hold on to her.

The queen slowly turned around, and he looked up at her: her ebony-black hair fell over her shoulders in sleek sheets, and her mauve cloak pooled around her dainty figure. She was perfection—all except for that black heart pulsating underneath her porcelain skin.

"I suppose I did say forever, and I don't break my promises, do I?"

She turned around and fondly stroked the mirror she had been admiring herself in minutes ago. She looked at him and then at the mirror.

"This will do."

"What do you mean?" he growled, his pain turning into fury. He felt the tears slipping. His eye twitched and his fists tightened. "You…you will pay for this!" he growled menacingly.

However, she hardly spared him a glance, still deep in thought staring at the mirror.

"Pay for what? You are a slave, nothing more. Who are you to threaten the queen?"

Her words sliced him open. This was his Anna, the woman who he had loved so fiercely these past few months. He had to believe she was still in there. He got up, and his eyes desperately roved up and down her body desperate to find one hint that this was the Anna he had fallen in love with. *Nothing!*

But he wouldn't give up. His crumpled forehead relaxed. He took her hand, and its familiar soft texture comforted him. Her eyes seemed to soften as she looked at him. But as William leaned in, a slicing sound cut through the air. He heard it before he felt it: the sound of a knife parting buttery flesh and the splash of crimson staining the floor. He looked down in horror to see the queen's once spotless hands now covered in blood gripping onto an itty-bitty insignificant shard of glass that had just torn his throat open. A mask, a lie!

He thrashed, but the realization that he had trusted her yet again stung him. He gurgled on his blood before going still…

Jamal snapped out of his trance and looked at the man who he now assumed was William. "That's it?" Jamal questioned, his mouth open.

William, in the mirror shard, shook his head. "I woke up in a mirror hours later. She cursed me so that when she died, I would too. I'm surprised I've survived this long. I was supposed to die the second she did. I can't seem to figure out if it's a mercy or a punishment." He chuckled bitterly.

"B-but that…that can't be, you—you told her to kill Snow White." Jamal feverishly attempted to validate his earlier thoughts about William and how he was evil.

"I know. That is one thing I do regret. Alas, I had no choice for she had cursed me with the inability to lie as well. I was so naïve." William breathed a sigh, looking ashamed.

For the first time in his life, Jamal was at a loss for words. Everything he had known to be true slowly crept away. He gingerly picked up the shard and cradled it close to him.

"I'm sorry," he whispered. "I didn't know."

William just shook his head, his face set in accepting his fate. "I just wanted to ask you one last thing," William said in a strong voice, a stark contrast to the tears running down his face.

"Anything," Jamal responded.

"Was I really evil or did I just fall in love with the wrong person?"

We All Fall Down

Allison Johanson

I don't think my parents meant to die young. I don't think our kingdom, Teresia, envisioned this happening when they wrote their laws. I don't think anyone meant to place the crown on the head of my brother, Roland, who is not yet six years of age.

But they did.

And now I, Amèe, as the eldest sister, am expected to carry the burden of my brother's throne.

After my classes are finished, I walk to my brother's room to see him after his recent trip to Areia with my sister Aubery, who is fourteen years of age.

I was unable to come along because I needed to study the politics of the nation. My sister Aubrey studies war and battles, and is responsible for the protection of Roland. He was visiting Areia to visit his betrothed and playmate, Johanne, as Aubrey and King Morris went over treaties and whatnot.

As I approach, I find the door flanked by two of the royal guard standing there, swords ready. They seemed awkward, waiting by the door to a child's room, but I'm thankful. When they see me, they nod respectively.

"His Majesty is waiting for you."

"Thank you." I smile at them as they open the door to let me in.

Roland sits cross-legged on his chair, reading an oversize book. His finger runs slowly under the words as he mouths them, a look of immense concentration on his face. Since he was crowned king, his learning has accelerated tenfold, and he's taught by only the best tutors in the kingdom.

I sit down next to him on the bed, placing a bowl on a nearby dresser. Brushing my dark, curly hair out of my face, I clear my throat and see Roland's hazel eyes rising to meet mine. He sets his book down, and we face each other.

"How was your trip?" Rolan looks down, not meeting my eyes.

"It was fine."

"*Obviously*," I say mockingly. "Now tell me, what's wrong?"

Roland looks away. "The Black Death is killing more and more people every day. And…Johanne has it."

My eyes widen. "No! Don't tell me it's true! You stayed away from her, right?"

"I didn't catch it from her! Aubrey got me this book to look for signs, and I don't have any!"

Roland tries to give me a hug, but I spring away.

"Get off! I don't want to catch the plague because of you! I'm going to go talk to Aubrey, while you try to get some rest. We can't afford you dying from the plague."

I run out of the room in a flurry of hurt and confusion.

As I head to Aubrey's room to talk to her, I'm shocked to see her knocking on my door, softly saying, "Amèe? Are you there, Amèe?"

All the anger I didn't even know I had fades. Aubrey turns to see me standing there, and she rushes to hug me.

"I'm so sorry, Amèe! I wanted to tell you as soon as we got back, but I couldn't find you!" She bites her lip nervously, eyes wide.

"It's fine…nothing we could do now. We just need to see what the future will hold."

Nevertheless, we spend the rest of the night finding people who might help prevent the terrible future awaiting us.

Johanne died of the Black Death.

Aubrey and I read the letter with increasing dread. Johanne was perfect.

Poor Roland.

After the letter arrived, he didn't want to leave his

room, preferring to live out the rest of his days sitting with his books about this horrid death.

He loved her. He would count the minutes until our parents could take him to Areia and he could play with her.

And now we can see the changes in him. Roland, like his father before him, might die from the plague.

The plague takes him in a firm hold. Every day he screams in pain, "It hurts! It hurts! It hurts!"

And I stand there powerless, unable to ease his pain, unable to bring peace to his troubles. He's terrified he might die. I'm terrified he's right.

Aubrey is in a state. No price is too high and no travel too far. Every day physicians, priests, apothecaries, and surgeons come in and do nothing.

The Black Death is supposed to last five days. Three have passed. Roland's coughing blood and running a high fever. Any food we try to feed him he throws back up. He is swelling, and with his tiny body, always small for his age, he looks misshapen and deformed.

My sister and I have stopped sleeping altogether. Our only hope is to do what we can, usher in each and every bloodletter with money in their pockets. It doesn't work. It doesn't help.

He screams in the never-ending, never-ceasing,

relentless waves of torture. He fears to come near the black mistress of death. He fears the time when the black mistress's suitor, the one in the crow mask, the one for sorrow, will knock on his door.

All I can do is hold him. All I can do is pick his tiny body up and whisper to him that everything's going to be okay. What's the plague anymore?

He doesn't scream when I hold him, even though we both know I hold him uncomfortably and it hurts him.

I sing to him too, songs I have heard small children sing. Even those are about the Black Death. *Ring-a-ring a Rosie, pocket full of posies, a-tishoo, a-tishoo, we all fall down.*

The Black Death is falling down on us like the vast curtain of sorrow, vanquishing everything in sight. It's taking over my life, and one day I'll have to yield.

I try to find an escape, where I can feel as if the Black Death isn't taking over my mind. To distract me from the pain coursing through my body.

Aubrey tells me I have a kingdom to run. She says now that Roland might be dying, I need to prepare to be queen. I try my best because I know we're both stressed—

But I can't. I can't do this. My head hurts, my

body hurts, it hurts, I can't breathe, it hurts, I can't breathe, I need help, no one will help, I can't, I can't.

Roland is dead. My brother is lying dead. I don't know what to do anymore. I wander around in a daze. I feel as if my very soul was sucked out of me. His death has created a hole in my chest that will never be filled. I wish it were me that died. He had something to live for.

Aubrey's doing what she can. She might survive this. I welcome death now. Death is an old friend. Death took my brother and parents. Death, black and bleak as night, fill my days with suffering.

I have succumbed to the Black Death. My days have become a blur. The bloodletting doesn't help. Aubrey tells me everything's going to be okay. It's not. I failed everyone. They were counting on me. Aubrey tells me she loves me. I try to smile. It hurts. I can't. I flap my arms uselessly, and Aubrey's hand holds mine, and I cry out. I don't want my perfect, loving sister to experience any more pain than what she has already suffered. I want with all my being for her not to get this horrid death.

I'm scared, Aubrey, I don't want to die. I said I'd welcome death, Aubrey, but I lied. I'm so sorry I lied.

I miss Roland. I miss my parents. I love you so

much, Aubrey.

I'm sorry I failed. I failed you, Aubrey. I failed everyone. People were counting on me.

I'm sorry I can't breathe, and I'm sorry it hurts. I want to tell you I feel fine. I want to help everyone. I'm sorry I failed at that, too.

I'm sorry.

I can't breathe.

It hurts.

I failed you.

I want to help you.

I'm sorry.

I can't do this.

I'm dying.

I'm scared.

I'm so scared.

I don't want to die.

Please don't let me die, Aubrey.

I need help, Aubrey.

Please help me.

When My Father Became My Hero

Seren Rifat

I used to think that hell was hot and fiery.

I'm now convinced that it's as cold as a Christmas day.

Even now, years after the Christmas of 1989, when that day became just a memory full of sadness, it's still hard to think back upon the events that made my father a hero…

It was because of a shortcut we took on the way home.

It was because Eastern Europe was trying to free itself from the chains of communism and build democracy on the ruins of an era that stole their joy.

It was because we happened to live right there, in the heart of the bloody revolutions, in Romania's capital.

Or maybe it was my grandma's fault.

Or maybe it was just suicide.

Or maybe I'm a criminal.

Or, or, or—

These are the only thoughts that my mind dwells on in the following months, years.

We were standing on the narrow hallway when I

asked my dad why he had to go. I was trying to stop him.

"I have to. It's Christmas, your grandma doesn't have any food, she can't move, she's ill… Should I continue?" He paused for a second. "The power of love is greater than the power of man."

The midwife then came out to us and propped herself against the door.

"You two can go. She said she doesn't want anyone in the room."

I could tell from the tone of her voice that she was exhausted.

"Alexandra's not coming. Too dangerous."

"It will take some time until your brother will be here." She looked at my mom lying on the bed. "Inhale, exhale, inhale, exhale…it will be over soon. I promise."

"How long exactly?" my dad asked.

"The contractions just started. It will take a couple more hours. I need to leave now. Take care out there," the midwife said in a rush. Then she disappeared out the wooden door.

My dad started to leave.

"Wait! I'm coming with you," I said while quickly putting on my red coat and leather boots.

I ran after him. He wasn't too happy about it, and looking back, I wasn't either.

We found my grandmother lying on her bed in a nest of blankets. The musty scent of my grandma's small communist flat invaded my lungs as we stepped inside. Old age slipped my grandma underneath its tongue and left her with heart problems and a paralyzed leg. Her face, caressed by the passing of time, brightened when she saw us; she cast a feeble smile in our direction.

"I didn't think you will come," she said, her voice trembling.

"We're not gonna leave you alone on Christmas day, are we?" my dad said, his upper lip bending in a smile.

Dad sat down next to her and kissed her hand, then he stood there with her hand in his. I stood beside the door.

"It's hell out there… You shouldn't be going out. I've already lived during a war, but I've never heard anything worse than what I heard today on the radio."

She paused for a second, then went on to tell us how she and her brothers had to stay in the basement for days during the war and only saw the light of the day when they went to in the garden.

I remember it well, the way my grandma used to tell little tales—that's what she called them—about her childhood, how she and her brothers survived in the countryside while the cities were being torn apart and how her father died after a series of bombs fell on the city of Bucharest.

"Elena made cabbage rolls. We brought you some."

My dad went to the kitchen, and I was left alone with my grandma. I didn't like to see her like that. It reminded me about the thought that used to haunt me every day—that she will be gone sooner than later. When you love someone, you'd do anything for them, and when you can't, when you are chained in front of time and old age, it's heart-wrenching.

"Tell your mom I said thanks for the rolls."

"I will."

My dad came back from the kitchen with a piping hot plate in his hands. He helped my grandma stand up and eat.

"We don't have any bread at home…and we couldn't find any at the shop."

It wasn't much of a surprise. There's never enough for everybody—not bread or any other food or toys or electricity or warm water. By the age of twelve, I was already used to this; I was used to helping my mother make a dinner out of nothing or my dad reading at the candlelight.

He liked reading. I used to lie in bed facing him and I always fell asleep with him reading Romanian tales. I could never forget the fragile flickering light the color of amber reflecting in his little reading glasses, which were always falling down his bumpy nose while he was sitting silently in his armchair beside my bed.

Before we left, I helped my dad wash the dishes, clean up the kitchen, and put everything in its place. I always admired him for this—there could literally be a war outside, but he would still come to visit his mom on Christmas.

Hand in hand, me and my dad made our way home among the sea of people. They were not revolting. They were celebrating. They were smiling and fluttering flags with holes in them.

Our breath was vapor; our cheeks were caressed by the wintry wind and red as if all the blood in our bodies rushed underneath our faces. It was one of those days when clothes felt thinner than they are. Upon the grass growing from the cracks in the pavement, there was snow, much like sprinkled sugar on the top of my mother's cakes.

At a corner, we turned onto a small path.

"It's shorter if we go this way," my dad said. "You're going to see your brother in a short while."

Fratele meu iubit. My beloved brother. I left the house thinking that my brother would be there, alive and healthy, by the time I came home.

He wasn't. When I came home, there was no baby

crying. The only cries were mine and my mom's.

BANG!

Beaming bullets burst around us like a thunderstorm.

BANG!

"Please stop! I have to see my little br—"

I fell.

My cheek was touching the frozen ground. Lying on the ground, my dad on top of me, I was screaming my heart out in the hope someone would hear me in the midst of the hellish chaos haunting the streets of our city.

"*Te iubesc.* I love you," my dad whispered in my ear.

BANG! BANG! I gave up screaming and started crying. Salty, freezing rivers flowed from my eyes.

BANG! BANG! BANG!

My dad screamed in pain.

They stopped. The men with weary faces who were shooting from behind a truck came toward us. They made me stand up, and I did as they said. I wasn't injured.

My breaths were short. My eyes were blurry with tears, but I managed to see the ruby-colored bloodstain on his coat.

This is my last memory of my father, when my father became my hero.

Demon of the Mind

Tia Mummau

Old Man Gregor walked to the ramshackle barn on the west side of his little farm as the sun rose above the mountains.

Gregor was stout, with thinning gray hair and a long white beard. He was a respectable man and had a good reputation as a farmer.

He was admiring the early morning sky as he walked down an old beaten path to start his day when he thought he heard something rustling in the bushes.

He stopped. Thinking it was his scraggly barn cat, Scruffy, Old Man Gregor called out to the bush, "Here, kitty, kitty, kitty! Come here, ol' Scruffy boy!"

The rustling stopped, but no cat came out of the bush.

"Hmm," he said aloud to himself, "that is rather odd."

The old farmer shrugged it off and continued down the path. After taking a few steps, he heard someone breathing heavily behind him. He turned around quickly, thinking someone was following him.

Nothing.

Nothing was there.

Rattled by the odd happenings, he quickened his pace until he reached the barn.

For the rest of the day, Gregor worked hard, tending to the animals and fields, feeding Scruffy and the mangy dog he called Max. Old Man Gregor worked so diligently he almost forgot about the strange things that occurred earlier that morning, though a few times, whenever he heard a loud noise, he jumped back a little.

After dusk, long after the warm sun sank below the mountains, Gregor decided that the day's work had been finished, as the animals rested in their pens. He grabbed a rusty oil lamp and headed back down the worn path to his home.

Now it was a rather ghostly evening, the moon was a full pale yellow, and the brisk October breeze swept through the trees with a small howl. Old Man Gregor cautiously looked around him, suddenly remembering what had happened that morning, when out of the darkness, he heard something breathing heavily behind him again, but this time, he felt an icy breath prick the back of his neck and seep into his spine.

Gregor stood, petrified.

He didn't know who it could possibly be. Gregor lived alone on the small farm with no ranch hands, and there were rarely any visitors.

Gregor shuddered as he felt something cold brush against his arm.

A gravelly low voice hissed in his ear, "*Come follow me and may your soul be spared from suffering. You have no one here. You're alone. So many bad things can happen tonight, don't you think? Come with me. Be my friend.*"

Old Gregor swallowed hard, "H-h-how will I follow y-you?"

"Follow the sounds of nature, if you want to be where pain disappears. Don't you want to be happy in the sunlight again? Or maybe you like the darkness? It is, after all, my home."

Gregor shook his head frantically. "No, no, no," he mumbled.

"You don't want to stay with me?" the voice hissed in a somewhat kind, alluring way. *"Stay in the dark. I can protect you from the outside world. Nothing will touch you or remember you're here. I will protect you and your farm."*

A rush of wind blew against the old farmer's side, and he shivered once more. He wanted to turn around, yet he was terrified at what could be behind him.

"Hmm, I see," the voice hissed in his head, no longer in his ear. "*You want to turn to see what's behind you? You want to know what I am? Don't you understand? I'm not behind you. Go ahead. Look."*

"W-what do you want from me?" Old Man Gregor turned around to be greeted by nothingness.

Gregor put his hand to his head, squinting his eyes and furrowing his brow. He felt an odd pressure in his forehead and sinuses.

The voice echoed in his skull, "*Oh, what's this? A memory I have found!*"

"Get out of m—" Gregor immediately grabbed his ears and screamed into the night. A screech rang in his ears until he couldn't even hear his own screams of pain.

The pressure increased in his head, and blood dripped from his nostrils, flowing into his mouth and down his chin.

Gregor crumpled to the ground, shaking in agony. His body went numb, and he could no longer feel the coolness of the autumn air on his skin.

"I think that is enough for now." The voice chuckled. *"Don't resist me. I am a part of you. Now let's see this memory, shall we?"*

The old farmer returned to normal almost as fast as the pain had overtaken him. He spat blood onto the dirt and wiped his nose on his sleeve.

Gregor looked around, frantically turning in circles, trying to spot the demon that was tormenting him.

He stopped spinning abruptly, feeling like he was paralyzed by something invisible.

Gregor's vision went dark around the edges, slowly tunneling until he saw nothing.

Flashes of memories flew past his eyes.

He saw himself getting bullied in school, getting beaten up by the bigger kids in his neighborhood. He saw himself being pushed out of a moving car by his father as a young boy and breaking his leg. He relived the moment his mother ran from his father as he chased her with a gun and heard the dreadful gunshot ring out right before silence echoed through the house.

He watched as he found a little abandoned girl, crying on his front porch, and then, he watched the same girl, that he had brought into his home, go blind and die of an incurable sickness before her life had ever really begun. All of these horrible things that he had tried to forget, things he had suppressed in his brain, came back. Tears of anguish spilled from his eyes.

Then the memories instantly stopped and his vision cleared, returning to normal.

"Well now, that was rather enjoyable! Don't you think?" the voice echoed inside the old man's head, sounding almost cheerful. *"I will ask you again... Will you stay in the dark with me now? I can make you forget it all. Come with me."*

Old Man Gregor, with tears and blood staining his face, spoke into the darkness, "You—you win. I want it to stop. I will go...with you. Where do I go?"

"Come with me to the cliff above the lake where the waterfall flows."

Gregor pulled himself up to his feet.

A strange noise came from the woods, and he followed it blindly in the dark of the night. He stumbled past trees and plants, until he came to a smooth flat rock that hung over a lake. He had made it to the cliff but was now regretting his choice to give in to his fear.

The rush of the water filled his ears, and the moon reflected off the lake.

"What do I do now?" Gregor said in a panicked tone.

"Take a white rock and write on the cliff, where you stand, anything you would like to leave for the knowledge of the world. Go on."

The old man got on his knees, scrambling to find a rock. His shaky hands fumbled around in the dirt until his hands wrapped around a small chip of limestone.

His hands shook furiously, and he dropped the chip a few times.

"YOU SLOW, STUPID MAN! WRITE IT ALREADY!" the voice roared in Gregor's head, making him jolt back.

He desperately scribbled, scratched, and scraped the limestone chip on the smooth cliff, recording a message that scared him.

When he was finished, Old Man Gregor dropped the limestone, sat back on his heels, and sobbed, crying out to the large pale moon, "What have I done? What has this world done to me? If there is a God, save me from my own demon!"

"STOP IT, YOU FOOL! No one can hear you! You know you deserve nothing and you mean nothing to anyone! Come stay with me in the dark, and your suffering will end for a time! Don't you want to get rid of me all the same? I can give you both."

"What must I do? Tell me!" Gregor's sobs were drowned out by the waterfall.

"Get up and go to the edge of the cliff."

The old man did as he was told by the demonic force that had taken over him.

"Now, jump, but when you do s,o jump next to the lake, not in it."

"B-but if I do that I will surely die!"

The voice chuckled. "*Don't you trust me?*"

"No! I did not want this!"

"Oh, you poor, pitiful man, I told you not to resist. I told you to follow me, to come with me, and you did. You wanted to be free of pain, and I offered it to you, but now, you dare reject me? There is a price to pay for your stubbornness."

The screeching ring returned to Gregor's ears and the painful memories of his past flew before his eyes again. The old man's vision went black, and he lost all sense of direction.

He violently clasped his hands to his head, screaming like a banshee from the depths of hell, as he dug his fingernails into his temples, screaming in pain.

Gregor stumbled as he shuffled his feet, desperately trying to move away from the edge of the cliff, but he couldn't see where he was going.

The old man felt his foot slip, and he viciously attempted to blindly regain his footing, but his attempt was useless and he only managed to fall off the edge entirely.

Weightlessly, he fell screaming in fear as he grew closer and closer to the rocky shore of the lake.

Gregor's screams finally ceased, and his voice was forever quieted as the waterfall roared on.

The only thing left of Old Man Gregor was his little forgotten farm, his broken lifeless body, and the message of horror he left behind scribbled on the cliff with limestone that read:

I have a demon inside of me, and it is myself.

The Street Urchin

Karuna Chandran

2001

Ding went my alarm as I waited by our house phone. Juniper had promised to call me every day at 9:00 a.m. once she had started her new job. It became somewhat of a routine for us to talk at that time.

Today, after waiting for five minutes, I was starting to get a little worried—Juniper always called right on the dot.

I had promised to meet my mom at IHOP for breakfast, and her break was from 9:15 to 10:00. I couldn't keep waiting for my sister to call. I tried to forget about Juniper not calling; her job was pretty intense after all.

Luckily, the IHOP was just five minutes away by subway, so I grabbed my subway card and hightailed it out of the house. I hoped my mom would remember our plan; often she got really carried away at work. I had to show up though, so that at least one of us would be consistent.

I got to the restaurant and quickly scanned for her. *Shocker, she isn't here! And she promised she would try harder.* I tried to shove the hurt down, but it kept resurfacing, like the feeling of eating too many pancakes.

I usually loved the subway because it felt like freedom, knowing that I could venture anywhere in the city with just a small ticket. On the other hand, today, as I clung to one of the grab bars, going back home, thoughts started rushing in like the Great Mississippi Flood. Maybe it was Juniper not calling me or my mom forgetting our breakfast plans, but the world just felt wrong today, like two puzzle pieces not quite fitting.

When I got off the train to go a different route, everyone I saw seemed to be acting hurtful and cruel. For example, two men were preventing an old lady from boarding the train. I also happened to see a mother yelling at her toddler to stop staring at a street musician and "get a move on." I even saw a lady push and shove people out of the way, just so she could get off the train. Everywhere I looked, people were insulting or snapping at each other. It didn't help that the air had a light smoky smell, as if it too had turned malicious.

How is this world so messed up all of a sudden? Or have I just been stuck in a bubble, too wrapped up with my own world to notice?

I got off at my station to board a different train. Even though I knew I should have been going home, I decided to sit on a bench (no one was expecting me back anyway) and soon became completely lost in thought.

"What are you doing?" said a sleepy voice.

It took me a second to pinpoint the sound. It seemed to be coming from…behind me. A small girl emerged, who had clearly been there for a while. She wore what looked like hand-me-down clothes, the color having seeped out of them a long time ago. Her raven-black hair, with all its tangles and split ends, reminded me of a sailor's knot. The girl's only possessions seemed to be an old ukulele, a small backpack, and the morning newspaper. However, out of all of those details, her eyes are what I remember the most. Bright green, like fresh morning grass. They were so vibrant and full of life, despite the dark circles around them.

"I'm so sorry! I didn't see you there, I was kind of…daydreaming," I said apologetically.

"No problem, but why were you daydreaming so much?" she questioned.

"Nothing, it's just that, I dunno, people seem so cruel to each other all the time. It makes me feel kinda helpless," I answered vaguely. After all, I had just met this homeless girl.

"Like who?" she pressed.

"I'm not sure if you saw, but two men were preventing an old lady from entering the train that I got off," I told her.

"Oh her, yeah..." replied the ragged girl.

"Also, did you see that mother scream at her toddler to get moving? Or that woman who shoved everyone out of her way just to exit. That's just not right!" I exclaimed. The air seemed to smell even smokier as I said that, as if in response to my anger.

"I did see all of those things. People do tend to notice negativity, as it is often a lot more boisterous and loud, commanding our attention. However, it is so much harder to realize all the quiet, unnoticed goodness around us."

"Like what?" I questioned.

"Like that lady at that burger stand over there. She always gives out free French fries to anyone looking hungry. Or that man over there, who's helping that girl put up her ad on the bulletin board because she's too short to reach it. Even that child, who's picking up the plastic straw and putting it in the trash, is helping out in his own unique way," she said passionately, the corners of her mouth lifting up into a smile the moment she finished speaking.

She's right! Why don't I see all these things?

"How are you so cheerful all the time?" I asked her incredulously.

"Am I? I guess I've learned to look on the bright side because it's the only thing I really have left. I've grown accustomed to living on the streets. While the New York subway is not the greatest place in the world to call home, after ten years, it has started to grow on me. I get to hear people as they pass by, getting on with their lives. And in a way, I get to play my small ukulele for the world. Whenever someone is disappointed or angry, seeing them smile in my direction somehow makes it just a little bit better," she told me.

Wow, she seems so wise beyond her years. I suddenly had an idea.

"Here's ten dollars. I was going to use it for pancakes, but since I'm going back home, I'd like you to have it," I said.

"See, always think positively. I didn't even have to play my ukulele and I got ten whole dollars just by talking. Maybe I should be a fortune cookie writer when I grow up!" said the street urchin, chuckling.

Seeing her grin made me smile.

"Hey, shouldn't you be at school?" I questioned.

"Yeah…but I haven't slept too well lately. My mom," she said, pointing to a lady in the distance, "needed me to help her out in the evenings. I just… needed the break today."

"But you have to—" I began. I wanted to tell her how important school was, but I was suddenly interrupted by her.

"Hey, do you smell that?" she asked me.

I realized that the faint smoky smell I'd noticed earlier had grown much worse. Soon enough, I heard hacking coughs all around.

What is going on?

Then I heard a loud voice. It was coming from the speakers in the subway.

"We regret to inform you that all of the subway lines are now closed," said the subway attendant.

Everyone around seemed in shock.

"What's going on?" I asked a woman nearby.

She ran, muttering something about hijackers flying planes into the Twin Towers.

Wait a minute, the Twin Towers? Oh my god. Juniper! No wonder she didn't call me!

"I've gotta go. My sister—she works in the North Tower," I explained to the homeless girl.

She replied, saying something like, "Don't worry. She'll be okay."

I was too worried to listen clearly. I had one last look at the girl with anguish. She may have come to terms with her life, but she had so much potential. I made a mental note to go back and find her.

Luckily, my home was only half a mile away. As I ran, the sky was orange tinted from the smoke. It felt like an apocalypse converging on the Big Apple, something that you read about in stories, but don't expect in real life. My heart started fluttering like a hummingbird's wings and I too started to cough. Luckily, a lady on the street was handing out bandanas from the store she owned. I gladly accepted one, and it did help filter out the smoke as I ran like the wind back home.

When I opened the door to my house, I saw my mom sitting on the couch. We shared a grave look, as I sat down next to her. After all I had gone through today, I barely remembered her missing breakfast. We then waited in companionable silence for Juniper to call. Now that I had stopped coughing, I realized that something else was bothering me, like an itch that doesn't go away.

What the homeless girl said to me before I ran off didn't quite sound like, "Don't worry. She'll be okay." It sounded more like.... "Don't worry. You'll be okay." But why would she say that?

And then it slowly dawned on me. I realized that for every one of those horrible, truly malicious people like the hijackers who destroyed the towers, there are countless kindhearted people who will rally together as a community and build from the ashes. I thought of the quiet, compassionate people in the subway, the street urchin who gave me valuable advice, and even the woman who was handing out free bandanas to help passersby like me.

"The phone's ringing, Bethany!" said my mom.

Sure enough, the ring cut the silence in the room. My heart was in my throat.

This moment could change everything.

But in the whirlwind of emotions that I felt, I never thought that I'd feel one of them—*hope.* It wasn't a promise, it wasn't an "it will be okay," but the street urchin gave me something more raw and real that I could hold on to. And I grasped it with all of my might.

Unordinary

Devanshi Bhargava

Year 2181…It's been three days since Mom's fallen ill.

I close the curtains, blocking out the panicked screams, ashy skies, and dystopian atmosphere of the world outside. Covering my mouth with a hand, I enter my mother's chamber to hand her a glass of water, the clear fluid being the only thing keeping her alive at the moment.

Weakly, she takes it from my hands and shakily brings it up to her lips. My heart hurts to see my strong, beautiful mother reduced to…to *this.* Pale skin, tinted green and gray. Dull, glazed eyes snaked with angry red veins. Covered in her own sick as her golden locks stick to her forehead, slick with sweat.

Could be worse, a small voice chips in my subconscious. *She could be dead.* That was true. Though no one quite knew how it started, an epidemic had wiped the nation. *Ninety percent* of the population had died from sickness, after being miserable for a couple of days. It was highly contagious and a miracle that I hadn't caught it by now.

Mom warned me to take Sam and go. But if I left, she'd die, and Sam didn't need that. It was only months ago that we received word that Dad had died in the war.

My little brother already lost one parent. If he lost another, I didn't trust myself to be the one to heal those wounds. We needed Mom. That's why she had to survi—

"L-L-Lucas…" It was a raspy whisper, but enough to arouse me from my thoughts. Drawing closer to my mother, I place a hand over hers, and her other one comes up to card through my golden hair. She smiles at me, before starting to fade away once more. "Go."

What? I stand dumbfounded, staring at her. But her look tells me that I hadn't heard wrong. Nonetheless, I question, "But why? Mom, you know I can't leave you li—"

I'm cut off by a scream. She's yelling, panting, twisting, and turning as she clenches and unclenches the sullied mattress. My mom's in pain, but all I do is back up. *The final stage,* I think as a numbness spreads in my chest. *She knew. She knew it was coming and that there was nothing I could do.*

I have to get Sam.

But no sooner does this thought form then Sam comes running in, having heard the screams.

"Mom!" he cries, rushing to hug her, to give comfort the only way a nine-year-old can.

He's going to get sick.

I try to pull him away, but he struggles against my grip. Amid my mom's cries of sheer pain, I can hear her pleas for us to leave. Until it stops. Sam and I freeze, watching with horror as our mother's body goes limp, and she lies unmoving.

"Sam," I say slowly. "We have to go. Now."

"No!" the young boy screams. "She's sleeping, and she'll be lonely if I leave."

My heart breaks seeing the way he clings to her, not realizing the truth. But I have to get him away. *I couldn't lose him too.* "Sam…come on. Let's go." I try tugging him away, only to find that the small boy won't budge. "You're going to get sick."

"I've been sick for the past week!" Sam retorts, snuggling closer to the dead body.

I stand there stunned.

What?

"Sam…" I begin, my voice gentle. "Why didn't you tell me?"

He shrugs in response. "Mom was worse. Besides, it was on and off anyways."

That's weird. I didn't think the disease did tha—

All of a sudden, Sam falls off the bed, and all color drains from my face. He's twisting and turning silently, face contorted in obvious pain. Spasms.

Or that.

I don't know what to do. So I hover around him, whispering reassurances I don't quite believe.

Suddenly, the spasms stop, and he collapses.

"Lucas…what…what happened?" he pants out, and all I can do is rub his shoulder while trying to make sense of this. Then his breathing quickens, and I'm aware of a light.

What the…

Both of us scramble up, and as I back away, Sam stares at his hands in horror.

"Lucas!" he screams, and I gape at his veins, fully illuminated and glowing *red*!

"I don't know…I don't know!" I yell back at him as my own heart rate doubles.

He throws his head back, and a eardrum-shattering yell escapes him as a beam of *red light* shoots into the sky. Then after a second, it's over as quickly as it began, and my brother collapses, staring at his hands as though they now hold some divine power.

But before I can speak, a large *bang* at the door resonates through the silent house, startling us.

"Stay here and hide," I tell Sam, who looks at me with doe eyes before nodding.

After making my way downstairs, I open the door to find three heavily armored government officials staring down at me. Gulping, I find my voice. "How—how may I help you?"

"Where is it?" the one in the front demands, piercing me with an icy glare.

"Is what?"

"The unordinary."

Unordinary? It takes me a second to process, and my mind flashes back to Sam's…*episode.*

"My brother?"

The guards launch into their explanation. "He'll need to come with us. Those who had…*side effects* to the disease will be sent to a camp for…*treatment.*"

The hesitation makes me uneasy.

"What are you going to do?"

"What we must," he replies, voice steely cold.

What does that mean?

It dawns on me.

They're going to kill him.

With as much courage as I can muster, I fake a smile. "Let me…let me go get him."

I run up the stairs, dashing into my mother's room, where I can just see Sam's blonde hair sticking out from behind the shelf.

As I shake his arm, he looks up frightened.

"Lucas! What happened? Why—"

"We have to go," I cut in, pulling him up.

"Go where?" my little brother asks, ripping his arm out of my hands.

I sigh, running a hand through my ashy hair.

"I don't know, Sam, but we *need* to leave."

How do I explain that he's in a lot of danger right now?

"And leave Mom?" he asks, gesturing.

"She's dead!" I burst out, and my heart aches as his playful eyes shatter, and he looks between me and our mother in shock.

"B-but…"

All of a sudden, there's a loud bang from downstairs. The officials have barged in. We're running out of time.

"What's going on?" Sam asks me, trying to comprehend.

"I'll explain later, but right now, we have to go. Jump," I say, pointing to the open window.

Sam's eyes widen as he backs away, shaking his head. "Are you crazy?"

I rush forward, take his hands in mine, and kneel down until I'm at his level. In his eyes, I see fear.

"Listen, Sam. Do you trust me?" A second goes by. His ice-blue eyes meet my sea-green ones. Sam's grip on my hands tightens as he takes a shaky breath.

"Yes."

I let myself smile. But another bang, this time on the stairs, snaps me out of this fantasy. "Then let's go!"

After leading him to the window, I take a final look at my mother's body. *I'll finally be the big brother you wanted me to be.*

We jump and roll for impact as we land in the shriveled grass.

"That was—" Sam starts speaking, but I quickly grasp his hand, pulling him up and placing a hand over his still-blabbering mouth as I look around. No one at the door, which means they are inside.

And we've got thirty seconds tops till they find us.

"We have to run."

Taking his hand once more, I head for the cover of the forest. I know of a fence on the other side. Once we cross that…we'll be home free.

Both of us tear through the overgrown brush and branches, gaining quite a few scratches here and there. But I don't dare stop running.

Finally, I see the metal structure. Pausing, I wait for a second to let Sam catch his breath.

"Up and over," I say, kneeling, giving him a boost.

He leaps over the fence, landing nimbly on the other side with me following.

I take a look around and finally allow myself to smile. There's a path. It leads over the hills, through some fields, and after that…well, I can't see any farther.

"Let's go."

And with that, I take Sam's hand as he silently pads along beside me.

I don't know where we're going. I don't know if they'll find us or what will happen if they do. I don't know why Sam *gliched* or what it means or when he'll do it again. But I do know one thing. We're family, and family always protects each other. No matter how *unordinary* they are.

The Summoner

Michael Sovyn

"RJ, please come downstairs for dinner! Hurry up. It's getting cold!"

RJ ignored his mom. He couldn't eat now. He was preoccupied with the HappyTime Summoner, a perplexing and wondrous machine that cost his family $6.4 billion to install. This futuristic device resembled a drinking fountain at first glance. But on closer examination, the machine was quite incredible. It sensed the emotions of an individual and created a temporary replication of what the individual desired. When the person was finished with whatever they created, it dematerialized. RJ and his family were one of the few lucky families that actually owned a fully functioning one.

"Robbie Joe!" His mom barged into the room, face red as a beet. "I called you ten minutes ago for dinner. What could you possibly be doing that's so impor… what is that?"

She gestured toward the overflowing pile of thousand-dollar bills in the corner, partially covered in a blanket.

"It's nothing, really," RJ began, but his mom cut him off.

"Are you counterfeiting again? I don't remember how many times I told you not to do that! You just wait till your father hears about this!"

RJ cringed. His father did not take punishment lightly. He would probably end up getting locked in his room for a couple of hours, as well as getting punished by his mom.

"You are hereby banned from using the HappyTime Summoner for anything, until further notice.

"But, Mom. I…"

"No 'buts,' young man! You must find different ways to entertain yourself. Now get downstairs and eat dinner!"

And with that she turned and marched out of the room, slamming the door behind her.

"I hate them!" RJ muttered to himself after dinner. "Now I can't even use the summoner to summon a game or something."

Instead, he was watching a TV show about a man named Ranger Jones who used poison gas to kill people.

"I wish I could get rid of my parents. Then I could be truly happy," he said to himself, not fully paying attention to the television.

Suddenly, a rather evil idea popped into his head.

"And I know just how to do it!" He snapped his fingers and bolted out of the room.

He forgot to turn off the television. And the ranger forgot about the poison he set and killed himself.

It was two in the morning when RJ dared to leave his room. He crept carefully down the creaking stairwell, ever so slowly approaching his goal. He slunk by the kitchen, the bathroom, his parents' room, and his family's pool. Finally he arrived at the summoning room: the resting place of the HappyTime Summoner. He flung open the door and knelt down next to the device, sitting there, lifeless and peaceful.

"I'm sorry I have to do this. I just need to get even with my parents."

He unscrewed the control panel and proceeded to destroy the machine. He cut wires and smashed buttons, laughing deviously all the while.

"This will teach them not to mess with me." RJ giggled as he plunged his wrench into the machine's mechanical underbelly. "And now to test it out," RJ said as he screwed the cover back onto the panel.

He thought of an apple. The machine flared to

life, beeping and flashing. Instead of an apple, however, it began to produce a thick, purple gas. A fly that was in the room passed through the gas and plummeted toward the ground. It lay motionless on the floor. RJ grinned triumphantly. He fanned away the gas, deactivated the machine, and hurried off to his room.

The next morning, RJ's parents decided to go out for breakfast. They also decided to let RJ stay home.

"Growing boys need their rest," explained Randy to his wife as they locked the door behind them.

RJ awoke to the sound of the car revving its engine and realized his parents were going somewhere. Completely forgetting what he had done to the HappyTime Summoner, he eagerly bolted to the summoning room.

"I can't believe they left me home to do whatever I want. Maybe they're not as bad as I thought."

However, when he finally arrived at the summoning machine, he noticed two things. One, the door was open to the room, and two, the lights were on.

"That's odd," RJ noted. "The summoning room is usually locked up tight. Oh well, I guess my parents used it before they left."

He walked into the room and began to think of thousands of dollar bills. The machine turned on but didn't begin to make its familiar humming sound. Instead, a purple gas began to come out of the machine, in small bursts. RJ suddenly realized why the lights were on and the door open. He tried to stay away from the gas, but it was too late. It surrounded his body. RJ could feel himself dying, his organs failing, one by one.

At that exact moment, he realized that happiness does not just come from the outside, but also from within. That relationships are an important part to a healthy life. He then thought about his family and what he had tried to do to them. Then everything went black.

About two hours after the accident, RJ's parents returned home from their morning coffee to discover RJ, lifeless in the summoning room, the now destroyed HappyTime Summoner behind him.

"Looks like we messed up on another kid," Jessica noted as she studied the sight of the accident.

"I think that he tried to kill us. I wonder what we did wrong this time," replied Randy.

"I guess I have to get the machine fixed again," said Jessica. "In the meantime, have Robbie Joe removed from the summoning machine room and put him with the others."

"I will do that as soon as I can."

"Oh, I forgot one thing. Can you release the next child from the coma chamber? I'm sure with this new knowledge we can finally get this parent thing right."

Debris

Nishta Nandakumar

It was 1974, the year Henry had finally learned how to factor polynomials. He sat at his dining table, brow furrowed and tongue sticking out, studiously finishing up his homework. The television blared in the background.

"Now, John, tell me," the newscaster asked from the television, "what can we expect to see coming from the ever-rising tensions between America and the Soviet Union during the Cold War?"

"Well, I don't know, David, but we might see war in the near future, especially after an American soldier killed Vladimir Anatoly, a revered Soviet general. It doesn't look great for us Americans anymore. It seems as though the USSR has had enough," John, the other newscaster, responded.

Henry looked up, eyes wide with curiosity, tongue still sticking out, his pencil still gripped tight in his hand. He had heard bits and pieces of this *event* from everyone, but his dad always distracted him somehow, not letting him near newspapers or the television because he saw him as "too young." Henry knew that his dad would never forgive himself if something—

anything—happened to his son after he had already lost his wife. What he didn't understand was that Henry wanted to protect both himself and his dad so that nothing like what had happened to his mom would happen to the two of them. The loss of her affected them both, and each showed their grief in a different way.

Henry craned his neck to see more, but his father came walking into the room and Henry had to turn away, back to his homework.

"Whatcha watchin' there, Hen?" his dad asked, concern and fear lining his voice.

Henry felt both a tingle of love for his father's concern and a stab of annoyance for his overprotective nature.

"Nothin', Dad," Henry responded, disappointed.

Just once, he wished he could get out of this little bubble his dad put him in to try and protect him from the bad going on in the world. But he was too scared to.

"Hey, Dad, can I go out to the store around the corner? I'm almost done with my homework," Henry asked, hope lilting his voice as he watched his dad consider.

He conceded with a sigh and a small shake of his head.

"Sure, Hen. Here." He reached into his pocket and pulled out some crumpled dollar bills, pressing them into Henry's hand. "Take this money and go have some fun. Remember though, be careful."

Henry's dad's eyes were solemn, almost as if he knew that one day, he would have to let go of his only child.

Henry was taken aback. He didn't think his father would agree. Elated, he all but jumped up from the table, but his father gripped his shoulder, not hard enough to hurt, but hard enough to make Henry look his father in the eyes.

"Hey, Hen, I know that I'm not giving you much space, but it's just 'cause I wanna protect you, all right?"

Henry nodded halfheartedly. As he ran out of the door, shoving the money in his pocket, he barely registered the "I love you" that his dad yelled at him, almost desperately.

Already out the door, pretending he didn't hear his father's words, Henry rolled his eyes. He shouldn't have to ask his father to go out or to watch the news. Was that really love? Henry didn't understand how could you love someone if you were spending all your time being scared about their well-being. There should be *some* time being spent on worrying about them, but not all of it. Not like his dad worried day in and out about him.

He kicked a wall, hard, and regretted it right after. Sucking his teeth and groaning, he ducked into an alley, hearing people whisper near him.

"Yes, yes, I know. We have to get out of here now before Vlad comes with the *thing*," a voice with a foreign accent rumbled.

Henry felt shivers down his spine at the tone of the voice. What was the *thing*? And was that a Soviet accent?

"Okay, let's go. I certainly don't want to get caught up in all that," a different voice with the same foreign accent responded, emitting soft laughter.

Could those men be Soviets? Didn't he just hear on the news that there could be a nuclear war brewing between them and the USSR? What was the thing they were talking about? After all, they both had many nuclear weapons in their arsenals. Or that's what his friends said. He wasn't allowed to watch the news. Henry's mind was spinning, mindless thoughts rushing numbly through it. He walked out of the alley quietly on shaky legs, not being able to shake off the nagging feeling that *something* was wrong. He shook his head, forcing himself to forget what he had heard so that he could enjoy his brief freedom. Walking to the convenience store, he was stopped by the sound of buzzing. He halted and swatted the air around his head. After all, it was a humid day in June; the bugs were everywhere. He shook it off and walked inside the store, looking around for something to buy—maybe some candy. But then the buzzing became a whine, which became a loud roar from a plane. A plane that was definitely not an American plane. Henry had known something was wrong, and he should have listened to that little voice in his head that told him to go back home.

"Hey, kid, I think it's best you come here and stay down!" the owner of the store shouted.

"I can't!" Henry yelled. He had to get to his dad.

Panting, he ran in the opposite direction of the planes. He burst into his house, and his father, looking crazed, all but dragged them as far away from the origin of the noise as he could, leading Henry through the orderly streets of their city, the capital of their country.

Later, they collapsed, exhausted, in the lobby of a government building—was it the Department of Treasury? Henry didn't know.

"Stay low," his father whispered.

Henry nodded.

And then he felt it.

It sent a shock through his whole body.

The building they were in exploded, and Henry

and his father were buried under the rubble. Everything was spinning. Why couldn't the world just hold still? Henry's eyes filled with tears that overflowed as he strained to look at his father, also in the same state. Henry reached out a hand to him, ignoring the searing pain in his body.

"I love you, Dad," he choked out, barely registering the pain and burning before the world turned black.

When Henry woke up in a blindingly white room in a blindingly white bed, he thought he had died. Blinking blearily, disoriented, he was taken aback when a chipper nurse came to his bedside to take his vitals and inform him that he had been unconscious for a while.

"So I'm not dead?" Henry croaked.

The nurse shook her head and hurried to get him some water. She asked him how he was doing, and with a scratchy, hoarse voice, he told her his limbs felt weird. She waved him off and said that was normal as they had been bandaged from severe bleeding and some third-degree burns.

Severe bleeding? Third-degree burns? What happened? Henry thought. The last thing that he remembered was reaching out for his father. His father.

Henry sat up with a jolt, wincing at the pain.

He started pelting the nurse with questions.

"Where's my dad? How long have I been out for?"

"You've been unconscious for three days," the nurse said, her alarmingly sunny disposition refusing to dim.

"What about my father?" Henry asked.

"Well, Henry, he's in surgery right now. His injuries were worse than yours."

Henry nodded, but his mind was riddled with fear and jumped to all the worst-case scenarios.

Was he going to lose his dad, the only person that cared for him? Where would he go if he did?

Henry remembered thinking that true love meant that you wouldn't worry about the person all the time. But now, he realized that he was wrong. The only reason he wanted to know what was going on was so that he could protect himself and his dad. And now, because of mistakes they both made, they were in this position. His dad loved him, too much. And Henry realized that he loved his dad too much too. Which was why they constantly worried about each other. Why was this happening? Why had he been so mean to his dad before? Henry absentmindedly tasted salt on his lips and realized that he had been crying.

Why should he and his dad have to pay for something that they didn't do? Shouldn't America have better security? After all, they went through the same thing during Pearl Harbor—a surprise attack.

Shouldn't they be better prepared now? And why did any country have to bring its innocent citizens into play? He, his dad, and tens of thousands of others who must've been wounded or killed from the nuclear bomb attack were all normal people. Henry was lucky enough to have survived. He was lucky enough to have been far enough from the site of the bomb that he wasn't killed immediately. But there were so many others that weren't—innocent people murdered in cold blood. They didn't sign up for war. They weren't part of the army. Henry admired the people who were brave enough to sacrifice themselves for people like him, but should all of this be stopping because of their strong army? His father didn't deserve this. He did nothing wrong. His father had spent his life trying to protect Henry, *loving* Henry, and now…now Henry might not have the chance to speak to him—or even see him—ever again. And he didn't even know if his father heard the "I love you" that Henry had breathed to his father during those last seconds before he was dragged under.

That night, he was woken from his restless sleep by a nurse.

The second the nurse woke him up, Henry knew that it was going to be bad news.

"Sweetie, I'm sorry, but your father has passed."

Henry doubled over as if he had been punched in

the gut. His father was dead. He half thought that this all was a delirious fever dream and that he would wake up, safe and sound, in his bedroom, and see his dad making breakfast in their kitchen.

And that's when it really hit him.

He would never hear his father's voice again; never hear the deep rumble calling him "Hen" affectionately, talking to his mother's wallet-size photo when he thought Henry couldn't hear him. Henry would even miss his overprotective nature. He would rather have had his father lock him in the house for the rest of his life. Because that would mean that he still had his father with him. How was this fair? He had to lose both parents? Henry's body racked with sobs.

He spent the rest of that night crying and cursing the Soviets, and the doctors who weren't able to help his father. He was even mad at both of his parents for leaving him. Why did this have to happen to him? Why was it his city that was attacked? The questions rolled around in his head like marbles. But mostly, he blamed himself. He blamed himself for not realizing how precious his time with his father was, how he was always mad at his father for protecting him. He hadn't realized how deep the love that his father had for him was. He wished he had realized that earlier. He wished he had made the best of what he had.

I Find Peace in the Rain

Megan Dustin

"I love you, my precious Dahlia," read the crumpled note written in perfect cursive handwriting. There were blotches from my tears. I folded it along the ripped creases and placed it in my trembling hand.

Stage 1: she is still here.

Her gray hair was curled perfectly to her body, frozen in the silver box. I looked at her as the pain flooded my memory. I would never wake up in her warm house with the smell of homemade cinnamon rolls ever again, but I refused to believe that was her body, lifeless and manufactured. The silver curls weren't natural, and her skin looked like plastic. My fiery red hair bounced as I turned around and ran out of the church sanctuary. The same church we had walked into every Sunday since I was four. She would walk beside me into the brick building, hand in hand. We would always sit in the third row and listen to the message from Pastor Todd. The tears flooded my already bloodshot eyes, and they stung my puffy cheeks as I ran out of the church.

I plopped down on the curb, took the round glasses off my blemished face, and rubbed the salty tears from my cheeks. The door opened behind me as Simon walked over. He sat by my side and put his loving arms around me. He said nothing; he just held me in his grasp. I thought back to all of the memories I had with Simon at her house. He had always found time to come to church with us. I pulled my shaking legs up to my deflated chest.

The door creaked open one last time as my older sister, Ivy walked out. The two of us always fought, but today she was just sad and tired. Her shoulders were slumped over, and her face was bright red. She looked defeated. Ivy sat next to Simon. He took one of his arms away from me and put it around her. All three of us together, sharing a communal sadness.

The service had finished an hour ago, and we were at home. A loud creek sounded as the door opened to the white ranch house I had lived in since I was two. The sun shone brightly, and the birds sang wonderful harmonies as if my life hadn't been ripped from my grasp just three days prior.

I stepped onto the front porch and took a deep breath. The warm air cut into my raw throat. I glanced over to the tree across the empty field of grass. Tears fell again as my feet began to pace toward the old oak tree. The tall, rough grass scraped my calves as my black dress flapped behind me. When I arrived at the clear, shady area, I fell to the ground. The memories poisoned my happiness and turned into anger. Grief had come to join my party of depression and anxiety.

Stage two: the fire burning inside me.

I hadn't slept in three days. I couldn't sleep, not without her here. My body had already been shutting down by the time I made it home from the funeral.

I tightened my fingers into a fist and punched the weeds surrounding me. I felt angry. Why did God do this to me? She'd done nothing wrong; I'd done nothing wrong! My eyes were dead inside, and my skin had turned paler than snow. I thought about the hole where my heart should be. The ugly pit in my chest was tightening and whirling like a tornado, sucking out all the air left in my weak lungs. My breathing became shallow and pathetic. I could no longer see, and my eyes were flooded by warm tears.

"I hate you!" I shouted into the empty sky as my voice became brittle. "How could you do this to me?"

But I didn't hate anyone because I could only hate myself. For not saying goodbye. I wasn't there for her. It was too late. I just wanted to see her face one last time, but I knew that wasn't possible. I wiped the tears away from my eyes and looked at a petite silhouette leaning on the strong tree trunk. Thoughts flashed through my sleep-deprived mind. I wiped my watery eyes once again and opened them. Nothing was there.

She wasn't there.

"I'm seeing things," I thought.

Rubatosis had suddenly flushed through my shivering body. My heart was beating a thousand times a minute. In just a short second, my heart was all I could think of. It felt nice to not think about the hole in my chest and know that I still had a beating heart. I hadn't realized that I had jumped up from the ground when I saw the shadow and began to fall back to the grass. I no longer felt angry. Just hopeful.

I stretched out my delicate body and looked up at the clouds. My thoughts began to wander. I strayed to the topic of clouds and how they brought us peace. We would stare at the magnificent shapes they displayed before us as they started to dissipate and crumble. Then we would run and hide in fear of the chaos and havoc they brought us. That was exactly how I had felt, beautiful, until my once-happy life crumbled to the ground in small shattered fragments.

"Maybe I'm crazy," I thought as I curled into a ball and began to let the tears drip from my lifeless eyes.

Stage 3: I'll do anything just for her to be here.

"Please let this be a horrible nightmare," I whispered to myself as if I had finally figured everything out. "Please don't let her be gone," I begged as the endless pit formed again. The tornado of pain and suffering.

The air in my lungs seeped out as if I was a deflating tire. I squeezed into a tighter ball as rain started to pelt down onto my feeble body. I used to hate the rain. The storms and thunder scared me, but when I was there on the ground crying, begging for her to come back, the rain felt harmonious. The rain reminded me of the storm raging inside me begging to be let free. I felt like water vapor cooling to form clouds that would soon cause a commotion. I realized there was nothing I could do to get her back; this was not a dream. This was my life. My life without her smile.

Stage 4: an emptiness that has taken control of my emotions.

I have no more tears. I feel numb and lifeless. Like an abandoned shell. It had gotten dark outside so I wandered up to the house with the rain still pouring. I wobbled up the steps, still in my black dress. I opened the door with a loud squeak to let everyone in the house know I had arrived. I slipped off my soggy white Converse shoes and made my way up the old staircase to my room, soaking wet.

I slowly made it to my yellow room, the third door on the left. The first room was navy blue and belonged to Simon, and the second was a light shade of aquamarine and belonged to Ivy. Both of those doors were closed.

I wandered into my darkened room and couldn't help but notice a shadow in the corner, sticking out like a sore thumb. This time I didn't blink and I refused to look away. The same petite figure was standing in the corner of my bedroom that I had seen outside at the oak tree. Without peeling my eyes from the silhouette, I switched on my lamp. She was gone.

I squeezed my eyes and waited for the burning tears to come, but instead, I just felt my throat close as a raging fire came through. I wanted it out, I wanted the pain to flood out of me, I wanted the storm of sadness to leave my chest, but it stayed. It sucked my emotions and the feelings I had left till was an empty balloon of a body.

I walked over and fell onto my bed and prayed I would fall asleep, but my mind was racing. I grabbed my laptop and searched "seeing dead people." I pressed enter and waited for the page to load. Once it came up, I clicked on the first link, but my eyes drifted up and I finally fell into my long-awaited sleep.

"Dahlia," she said.

I noticed her silver curls; they were real. Her skin was pink and alive.

I ran over to her and held her tightly in a hug and sputtered out, "I'm sorry I wasn't with you."

"It's okay. I love you, my precious Dahlia."

I jerked awake and grasped her note, and I read it over in my head.

"I love you, my precious Dahlia."

About Lune Spark Books

Lune Spark Books aims to encourage children to engage in creating writing. We work with parents and young writers to promote creative fiction writing to help identify talent. We run annual competitions and creative writing classes and publish short stories by the young writers. For more details, visit us at http://lunespark.com/youngwriters/.

For the details of the contest or to enroll in the contest, please visit us at
http://lunespark.com/youngwriters/storycontest/.

Follow us on social media to keep up with the latest updates:

https://www.facebook.com/youngwriterscontest/
https://twitter.com/LuneSparkLLC

Other Anthologies by Lune Spark

A Window to Young Minds *(Age: 10+ years)*
This book is the first of the Lune Spark Short Story Contest's yearly anthologies and includes twenty-five award-winning short stories by young writers.

The Emotional Embodiment of Stars *(Age: 13+ years)*
Wonderfully wide-ranging, original, and enjoyable, this outstanding collection features twenty-seven short stories like *Mortimer*, in which an unwanted guest secretly follows a family through their heartbreaking sorrows.

Speaking Up for Each Other *(Age: 10+ years)*
Wonderfully wide-ranging, original, and enjoyable, this outstanding collection features twenty-four short stories like That Glowing Penny, in which a helpless girl has to live in fear of her own family.

Just One More *(Age: 10+ years)*
A collection of twenty-nine award-winning short stories by middle grade children. These stories encompass a wide range of genres, inviting readers to explore a wealth of important themes passionately crafted by these young writers—from a beautiful dragon called Ephyral giving up her freedom to save her entire species to a fifteen-year-old girl named Louisa Brixham dealing with her brother being accused of a crime she committed.

www.ingramcontent.com/pod-product-compliance
Lightning Source LLC
Chambersburg PA
CBHW050525190726
48284CB00003B/948

9781947960367